OF
THUNDERBOLT

A DEPARTMENT 89 NOVEL

MARK O'NEILL

PRAISE FOR THE DEPARTMENT 89 SERIES

"This whole series is a delight. I had to rush back to Amazon and buy up some more of O'Neill's books."

"Exceptionally well written, a pleasure to read and highly recommended to anyone looking for good reading."

"It's not often that I am so enthralled with a story that I read the entire book nonstop in one sitting, but it happened here."

To Monika and Schlumpf, my muses.

Also to the singer Billy Ocean, whose albums on continuous loop helped me over the finish line to finally get this book out. When the going gets tough, the tough write a book.

CHAPTER ONE

Paderborn

Mikhail Kharkov was starting to have serious second thoughts about the job he had agreed to do. As the battered truck he was driving sped along the darkened Paderborn streets with its illicit cargo in the back, he wondered, not for the first time, if he should have at least demanded more money.

But that was always Kharkov's problem. He was too impulsive, too quick to say yes if banknotes were flashed in front of his eyes. If he saw money, his brain switched off and common sense suddenly didn't apply. He didn't have the impulse control to say no, or at the very least to think the matter through to its logical conclusion. If he had done so in this instance, he would have immediately calculated that he would be taking an enormous risk for a very small reward.

He sighed at his lack of foresight. It was too late now. His only option was to finish the job by delivering the truck to Dortmund, walk away quickly, and forget about what he had done, if that was possible. He instinctively crossed himself then wondered why he had bothered. He was already convinced he was going straight to Hell when his time came. Most likely, God had given up on him a long time ago as a lost cause. His parents already had.

His thoughts were interrupted by flashing blue lights ahead on the darkened road. Squinting his eyes, he could gradually make out the outlines of a police roadblock. His heart sank.

"Damn!" he muttered, his shaking hands gripping the steering wheel so tightly that his knuckles started to go white.

So close to Dortmund. The chances of getting through the roadblock if they decided to check the back was impossible - and what kind of a police roadblock didn't want to check the contents of a vehicle?

But a shootout with the cops? Even though he was armed, the thought of firing on a police roadblock, and them firing back, was extremely unappealing. He had no desire to die and equally no desire to spend the rest of his life in prison for murdering police officers.

Then he thought '*are they looking for me?*'

He immediately waved aside the thought. The stakes on this job were too high for anyone to inform on him to the police. Everybody knew who he was working for and nobody had the guts to turn against *him*.

He lowered a hand slowly and tapped three times on the wall behind his seat. That was the signal for the police approaching so those in the back knew to be quiet. A discreet knock back confirmed that he had been understood.

Kharkov decided it was just a random roadblock and he could most likely bluff his way through it. His hands started sweating at the thought and he instinctively wiped his palms on his grubby jeans, as he slowed down in front of the police checkpoint. Kharkov saw an officer raise a hand and come forward, flashlight in the other hand.

Another two were standing at the barrier. Kharkov could see none of their faces because of the darkness. He wound his window down and the cold night breeze hit him in the face, making him flinch. The officer with the flashlight walked up to Kharkov's open window and nodded.

"Evening sir" said Wolfgang Schmitz, "cold night to be out."

Kharkov nodded nervously. "Yes, you're right. Quite cold."

"That must explain why you're shaking then" said Schmitz, "licence and registration please, and make it quick. My boss is watching and it's performance review time. Oh and please turn your engine off. It's bad for the environment."

"Yes, yes of course" said Kharkov, fumbling with his documents and turning the ignition off. *What was wrong with him?* This was not his first police checkpoint and it certainly wouldn't be his last. But right now, he was shaking like a coked-up squirrel on a dance floor.

As he handed over the documents to Schmitz, he could feel the reassuring bulk of his pistol tucked into the back of his jeans. Thankfully it was concealed by his jacket so Schmitz currently couldn't see it.

"So where did you start off from?" asked Schmitz, examining the documents.

"Katowice" said Kharkov irritably, "that's in Poland."

"I'm well aware where Katowice is" said Schmitz, calmly, "and what is your final destination?"

"Dortmund."

"Lucky you" said Schmitz, "you'd have to pay me to go anywhere near Dortmund."

"I *am* being paid" said Kharkov, "can I go now?"

Instead of replying, Schmitz's gaze wandered to the back of the truck. "What have you got in the back?"

Kharkov struggled to steady the sound of his voice. "I don't think I need to tell you that. I've done nothing wrong, unless driving in the middle of the night is suddenly a crime."

"So self-righteous. Everyone's a lawyer these days"

said Schmitz, cynically. "I blame all those legal shows on TV...."

WHILE SCHMITZ KEPT KHARKOV busy at the front of the truck, Major Sophie Decker was stealthily making her way to the back of the vehicle.

She had taken advantage of Kharkov looking out of his left-side driver's window at Schmitz and she had come through the bushes on the right. She was now standing at the back door of the truck, a flashlight in her mouth, while she used a lock pick on the padlock which kept the doors securely fastened together. As she worked, she could hear Schmitz continuing to talk.

"Russian are you? I had a Russian in my family. Hundreds of years ago, though. Had a fling with a Tsarina. Total alcoholic. Had vodka in his veins instead of blood....."

Decker smiled to herself. Schmitz could talk for Germany. Kharkov wasn't going anywhere soon. Schmitz knew she was back there and he would distract Kharkov for as long as it took.

The padlock eventually clicked open and Decker carefully removed it. But when she tried to remove the chains, they made too much noise and Kharkov heard it.

"What the hell?" he yelled and instinctively reached for his gun.

Schmitz suddenly had his own gun in his hand and calmly pointed it at Kharkov's head. "Don't move an inch my friend or the contents of your head will be all over the windshield. And if that's a gun you've got behind the door, pass it over - carefully."

But before Kharkov could hand over the weapon, he and Schmitz heard the loud boom of a shotgun coming from the back of the truck - and women screaming.

Schmitz looked to his right. "Major?"

Kharkov took advantage of Schmitz's temporary distraction and pulled his own gun out from his waistband. Firing once, the bullet missed the side of Schmitz's head by millimetres. Shocked, Schmitz dropped his weapon and fell backwards onto the ground, dazed.

As Sergeant Penelope Brinkmann, the third person at the checkpoint, rushed forward, Kharkov slammed his foot down on the accelerator and the truck rushed forward. It smashed through the checkpoint and a gunman fell out of the back of the truck.

THE MAN that fell out was the one holding the shotgun. It was his job to keep the women in the back quiet, especially if they encountered a police checkpoint. It was also his job to deal with any nosy people who thought to pick the door lock to take a look in the back. The women were being transported into forced prostitution in his employer's brothels, so they were worth a great deal of money.

Which was why he had immediately fired when he heard the padlock and chains being removed from the door. His boss had made it plain he was to fire first and maybe think of asking questions later. Thankfully for Decker though, his aim was as bad as Kharkov's, and the shot went right over Decker's head. But she still fell backwards in shock from the force of the blast.

Meanwhile, one of the women had decided to take advantage of the sudden open door, and in a burst of determination, she had pushed her captor out onto the road. He hit his head hard on the road on impact and was knocked unconscious.

Kharkov for his part didn't get very far. After smashing the police car out of the way as if it was papier-mâché, he was about to put on speed. But Brinkmann ran up to the front of the truck, aimed, and fired one shot into the windscreen. The bullet hit Kharkov in the throat and he clutched the wound as blood pumped through his fingers. With both hands now off the steering wheel, the truck spun sharply, left the road, and hit a muddy ditch. The women in the back screamed as the back doors flapped about wildly. Steam rose from the ruined engine.

"Major? Captain?" said Brinkmann, still pointing her MP5 automatic weapon in front of her, "talk to me."

"I'm dying" moaned Schmitz, lying in the road, "the shot missed my ear by this much. I have beautiful ears."

"And my ego is mortally wounded" muttered Decker, crouched on all fours in the middle of the road, "how did I not know they would have someone in the back? I'm really getting old."

Satisfied her colleagues were not bleeding to death, Brinkmann got out her mobile phone and texted a pre-arranged code back to headquarters, indicating that the incident had gone pear-shaped and they needed urgent assistance. She then ran to the truck. The women were still in the back, looking dazed.

"Stay in the truck!" shouted Brinkmann in English, "you are safe but you must stay where you are."

Without waiting for a reply from any of them, Brinkmann then slowly moved forward, her gun pointed straight ahead. She found Kharkov, half out of the driver's door, choking on his blood, his eyes bulging. It was obvious that he had seconds left to live. He looked at her pleadingly, his blood-soaked hands extended in some sort of plea for help, as he gurgled blood.

"Damn, the Major's going to have my ass for this" she whispered furiously, "she wanted him alive."

The sound of police sirens made it clear that the real police were about to turn up. As the first police car screeched to a halt, Kharkov chose that exact moment to breathe his last breath and his hands fell to his sides, his eyes wide open.

THE POLICE WERE CONFUSED to find three people dressed as police officers. They immediately assumed Decker, Schmitz, and Brinkmann were colleagues.

"I need to see some identification" said one of the officers, holding his pistol.

"We're government agents" said Decker, limping up. She had the semi-conscious gunman in flex-cuffs. "Put your guns down and help those poor women out of the back of the truck."

The officer looked at the truck, where some of the shaken women were peering out, fear on their faces.

"I still need to see identification" said the officer, stubbornly.

"Call Chief Inspector Otto Busch of the Berlin police" said Decker, "he will vouch for us. My name is Decker. I can guarantee you'll hear a string of obscenities when you tell him my name."

As the officer got out his phone to call Busch, Decker got the distinct impression that the officer already knew her by reputation. The look on his face said it all. Moments later, the officer returned, a pissed off look on his face. He turned to his colleagues. "Guns down. They check out. Bloody spooks."

He looked at Decker. "You're right. Chief Inspector Busch hates your guts. He also wants to know why German Intelligence is getting involved in what is clearly an illegal smuggling ring. He thinks you're...

quote...'sticking your big nose where it doesn't belong - *again*'...unquote."

Decker glared for a moment. "Follow me."

The officer hesitantly followed Decker who walked up to the truck. "Everyone out!" she shouted.

The women looked at each other in confusion then slowly got out.

Decker looked at the police officer. "You want to know why we're involved tonight?"

She got into the back of the truck, glanced at the sides then grabbed an automatic rifle that Schmitz reluctantly handed her.

"Because of this" she said.

She used the butt of the rifle to smash the sides of the truck. Eventually, hidden compartments were revealed. Inside each compartment were neat stacks of plastic explosives and detonators packed tightly inside.

"They were not only sex traffickers. They were also terrorists" said Schmitz who had a hand firmly on the shoulder of the gunman who was slowly recovering and looked thoroughly sullen, "those explosives were on their way to ISIS groups here in Germany."

"You're welcome" said Decker throwing the rifle to the stunned police officer as she jumped down to the ground, "don't mention it."

CHAPTER TWO

At the same time that Kharkov was meeting his sudden and violent end, a small plane landed at a private airfield outside Berlin. After it taxied to a halt, the door opened and a man looked out. He sniffed the air as if he was a bloodhound searching for a scent, and then, seemingly satisfied, he walked down the steps onto the tarmac.

His colleagues followed behind carrying bags and equipment, but he didn't. Privileges of rank, he thought. People like him did not carry things. That was why he had flunkies. He arrogantly stepped onto German soil as if he owned the place and flexed his shoulders.

It had been a long flight and he would not have accepted the job if he had not been given a direct order by the CIA director himself to get on the plane. He had been handed a Top Secret file with the name "Operation Thunderbolt", told who his team were, and that the plane was waiting at the airport. At first he was angry to be ordered about but when he started reading the file on the plane, his mood suddenly changed.

He was going after President Trent's assassin. He was going after *her*.

As the plane had sped across the Atlantic Ocean, Agent Tom Finn obsessively looked at the covert surveillance photos of Major Sophie Decker. Memorising every part of her face. This was the woman he was ordered to kill, along with every single member of her department. The CIA wanted Department 89 obliterated and a message sent to Chancellor Meyer.

Finn and his team were the messengers.

The message? You don't mess with the CIA and expect to get away with it.

As Finn and the others flashed their fake diplomatic passports at German airport security officials, he thought back to his meeting earlier with the CIA director.

NORMAN LESTER WAS SITTING at his desk reading the Washington Post and drinking strong black coffee. As Lester read an editorial and snorted with derision at the editor's high-minded tone of voice, his desk intercom buzzed. He jabbed the button.

"Yes?"

"Agent Tom Finn is here as you requested" said his secretary.

"Good. Send him in" said Lester, jabbing the button again which cut the connection.

A moment later, there was a knock at the door, and Finn walked in. Lester immediately sized him up. He had heard a lot of things about Finn - a lot of it good, but also a lot of it bad depending on your point of view. Lester wanted someone ruthless to do the task he had in mind, but he had to be sure he wasn't giving the task to an out-of-control ticking time bomb.

"Agent Finn" said Lester, "come in please. Sit down."

"Thank you sir" said Finn, gruffly. He looked exhausted and haggard, and a three day stubble of growth was on his face. This did not go unnoticed by Lester.

"Do we not pay our agents enough Agent Finn?"

"Sir?"

"You seem to be unable to afford razor blades. You come to a meeting with me looking like you've slept in a dumpster overnight."

Finn fought to contain his mounting irritation. "With respect sir, I have just got back from an op in Columbia. I had literally ninety minutes sleep before your secretary called me and told me I had thirty minutes to get here to Langley to see you. Grooming couldn't be squeezed into the tight timetable."

Lester sat back and studied Finn closely. "You know, I've heard a lot of good things about you Agent Finn.

Very good things, like how you get the job done no matter how distasteful. On the other hand, I also hear you have a temper problem, a drink problem, a problem with authority, and that you are a borderline psychopath. Would that be a fair assessment?"

Finn smirked. "I wasn't aware that the CIA only employed choir boys. As long as I get the job done, who cares how some shrink diagnoses me?"

"At the end of the day, I don't care" said Lester, "but I do need to know that my agents out in the field - especially the ones who are off-the-books - are not going to go all half-cocked and off the reservation. Can I rely on you to show self-control and stay on mission?"

"Have I ever failed in a mission yet?"

"There's a first time for everything Agent Finn" said Lester, tossing a manilla folder across the desk. Picking it up, Finn immediately noticed the "Top Secret" designation and the name of the operation underneath.

"Operation Thunderbolt?" said Finn, "someone's being a bit theatrical around here."

"Read the dossier on the flight" said Lester, "your team is already on the plane waiting for you. Wheels up in thirty minutes. You'd best get going."

"I prefer to either work alone or choose my own team" said Finn, sourly.

"You'll do what you're told." said Lester coldly, "that will be all, Agent Finn. I expect updates every twenty-four hours. Please don't make me send over another team to rein you in."

As Finn left the office with what he thought was another bullshit assignment, he idly flipped open the folder and looked at several photographs sitting on top. Attached was a piece of paper with the typewritten command.

KILL THEM ALL

DAYLIGHT WAS BREAKING in a Berlin suburb when Sophie Decker suddenly woke up in a strange bed. Her eyes shot open and her adrenalin started to kick in as she tried to quickly figure out where she was. Then she remembered.

Briefly closing her eyes with dread, and taking a deep breath, she turned and looked behind her. There lay Penelope Brinkmann, lightly snoring.

Decker looked under the covers, realised they were both naked, and put two and two together. She looked horrified at her lack of good judgment, letting out a silent scream.

"Oh shit no" she muttered and frantically started looking for her clothes, "no, no, no."

The sudden shift in the bed, and Decker's muttering

roused Brinkmann who blinked and looked at Decker, alarm on her face.

"Yeah I knew this was a bad idea when we ended up back here last night" said Brinkmann.

"A bad idea?" said Decker, "That's putting it mildly. I'm your superior officer. If word of this gets out, I could be court-martialled for fraternisation. Where the hell are my jeans?"

"Probably in the hallway" yawned Brinkmann, "you can relax Major, I'm not going to tell anyone and I'm sure you won't either. It'll stay between us."

Decker glared. "If you believe that, you'll believe anything. These things always get out. Schmitz for one is not an idiot. He can sniff these things a mile away. He's a bloodhound."

"Better come for a shower then, to wash the scent off" said Brinkmann.

"No, I'm going to the office" said Decker pulling on the last of her clothes, "and in case it needs saying, this was a one-time thing."

Before Brinkmann could respond, Decker had grabbed her holstered gun and jacket, and was walking to the door. As the door slammed shut, Brinkmann sighed.

"Make a girl feel wanted, why don't you?"

AS DECKER WALKED OUTSIDE into the early

morning light, the cold air hit her in the face and she shivered. Zipping up her jacket, she cursed her own stupidity.

She had been in the military long enough to know that what she had done that night was both monumentally stupid and a career-ender if it ever came out. But both she and Brinkmann had been completely buzzed after the incident with the truck and one thing had led to another.....

Normally when Decker felt like this, she worked it off with alcohol. To her, sex was not that important. For her, the job was her substitute for sex and she was embarrassed to admit to herself that she almost got a sexual rush from kicking the asses of bad guys and getting away with it.

But last night, she realised how attracted she was to Brinkmann and that she had felt that way for quite some time. She couldn't remember who had initiated things but one thing was for sure. If push came to shove, the buck would stop with her as the department chief. If heads rolled, it would be hers. Kicking the wall in anger, she turned and walked away down the street, her hands in her pockets.

As she walked away, she was being watched by four men in a car on the opposite side of the road. One of them was Finn.

"Well that was an unexpected bonus" said Finn, lighting a cigarette. "Who would have thought Decker was into screwing her subordinates? Female ones as well. We'll have to file that away for another day in the 'just in case' file."

The others nervously chuckled.

"Do we take Decker now?" one asked.

"No" said Finn, "for one, she isn't an idiot and is likely to shoot at least a couple of you dead before we maybe end up getting her ourselves. And second, she's the cherry on the cake. She comes last. I want her to see her precious department slowly getting taken apart, piece by piece. Then I will personally put her out of her agony but not before a long drawn-out torture session."

"So what do we do now then?" asked another.

Finn gestured to the building opposite. "Take out Brinkmann. And make it *very* messy."

CHAPTER THREE

Brinkmann turned off the shower, opened the cubicle door, and wrapped a towel tightly around her body. She then put on a bathrobe and began to vigorously dry her hair, walking into the bedroom as she did so, mindlessly humming a tune.

She was really pissed off and now she understood why. It wasn't the rejection by Decker that stung. It was the fact that Decker was right. What they had done was extremely stupid by anybody's standards.

But people in their line of work never had the chance for a 'real life'. So their chances of being able to pick someone up for a one-night stand was virtually nil. After all, you never knew if that person was an innocent civilian looking for a one-night stand, or a foreign agent sent to kill you or compromise you in a honeytrap.

Throwing the towel on the floor, Brinkmann started

to walk back to the bathroom. Then she heard the squeak.

She knew the stairs outside were squeaky but they were *all* squeaky. So one squeak was not normal. If a neighbour was coming up the stairs, she would be hearing a whole succession of squeaks by now.

But only one?

That to her meant only one thing. Someone was coming up the stairs who hadn't known about the squeaky steps, and was now standing absolutely still, figuring out what to do next.

Brinkmann opened the cupboard in her bedroom, reached into the back, and carefully removed a black scuffed machine gun. She also picked up her standard Department 89 panic button, issued to all operatives, and put it in her bathrobe pocket. She would only use it when she was sure she was actually in danger. She would be in big trouble if she hit the button without needing to.

Checking to make sure the gun was properly loaded, she stood to the side of the bedroom door. She pointed the gun at her front door, making sure she was out of the line of fire if somebody blasted through the door. She tried to steady her breathing, which jumped again when she heard another squeak, then another.

Whoever it was was now moving, and at that speed, it sure wasn't 92 year old Mrs Hartmann from the floor above. She raised the gun even higher and took aim so whoever came through the door would get it directly in the chest. She just hoped Mrs Hartmann or any of her neighbours would not choose that moment to come back with their groceries.

Brinkmann had made the mercury-tipped hollow point bullets herself and knew that just one of them would cause very serious damage to an opponent, if not kill them outright.

The squeaking stopped. Then the door handle slowly started to turn.

Brinkmann knew right then that she really was in danger. She reached into her bathrobe pocket and pressed the panic button. No sooner had she done so than a loud boom shattered the wood of her door and she instinctively lifted a hand to shield her face.

———

DECKER WAS ABOUT to fire up her motorcycle which she had left several streets away from Brinkmann's apartment when her phone rang. She briefly thought about ignoring it but then realised she couldn't. It could be anyone about anything. Ignoring the call was not an option.

"Yeah, what?"

"Major, it's Liebermann. We've had a panic alarm set off at the home of Sergeant Brinkmann."

Decker's heart stopped. "A panic alarm? But I've....."

"What?" said Liebermann.

"Never mind" said Decker, "I'm in the area. I'll check it out. Send backup just in case I need it."

"Do you need the address?" said Liebermann, but she realised Decker had already hung up.

Decker revved her motorcycle engine and swung around back in the direction of Brinkmann's apartment.

———

WHEN THE SMOKE and dust settled, Brinkmann saw a masked man emerge through the door. He was armed with an automatic rifle and was momentarily confused by the smoke which was partially obscuring his vision.

Brinkmann didn't hesitate. She raised the machine gun and fired a short burst, which was immediately followed by the man's chest exploding. His corpse flew backwards from the force of the blast into the wreckage of the doorway, and the one behind him stumbled as he tried to step over his dead colleague.

Brinkmann tried to fire again but the gun suddenly jammed. Unable to believe her bad luck, she threw the useless gun down and ran across her bedroom. She ran around the bed, yanked open the bedside cabinet drawer and pulled out a Glock handgun.

Rolling on her back, she saw the next gunman come into the bedroom. Before he could fire, she kicked the underside of her bed with her bare foot, causing pain to arch up her leg. But it made the bed topple over crashing into the intruder's shins. It only stopped him for a second by making him lose his balance and stumble back. But it was enough for Brinkmann to fire two close precise shots into his chest. He shrieked with pain, his legs buckled, and he crumpled to the floor.

The third gunman however was not so quick to come into the room. He saw his two dead colleagues on the floor and very quickly decided he wasn't going to join them wherever they were headed. Instead, he poked his gun around the door and sprayed bullets randomly around the room.

Being on the floor, a lot of the bullets flew over Brinkmann's head. Some shattered the windows but most thudded harmlessly into the wall, causing chunks of plaster to crash onto the floor.

Brinkmann's luck suddenly ran out and she was hit. One bullet hit her in the arm and another in the hip. Bleeding profusely, she tried to hide behind the bed but she knew that her handgun and wooden bed were no match for an automatic rifle. She lay on the floor in severe pain as bullets continued to fly, hoping for a miracle.

Little did she know that the miracle was coming.

CHAPTER FOUR

Decker continued to put on speed as she got closer to Brinkmann's apartment. She could hear loud bangs and as she turned the corner into Brinkmann's street, she saw the bedroom window shatter and shards of glass hit the street below.

On the other side of the street, Finn sat in the car and fumed. As he had suspected, Lester had given him a bunch of imbeciles for a team, and three of them were either dead or about to be captured. He grabbed the butt of his pistol, wondering if he should just go over now and put a bullet in Decker while he had the chance. But the sound of incoming police sirens convinced him that he had to leave while the going was good. Decker's fate would have to wait.

Cursing heavily under his breath, Finn started the

car and slowly drove away. If any of Lester's idiots survived, they were on their own.

———

DECKER SCREECHED to a halt outside Brinkmann's apartment building, threw the bike to the ground and ran inside with her helmet still on. Pulling her gun out, she bounded up the stairs two at a time and arrived at what remained of Brinkmann's front door. The sight of the first body made it clear that a vicious gunfight had just taken place.

Stepping inside, she made it to the bedroom to see another gunman point his weapon at Brinkmann. Without thinking, Decker rushed forward and slammed her gun into the back of his head. He grunted and fell forward onto the overturned bed where he lay unconscious.

Running around to the other side of the bed, Decker saw blood all over the floor. Then she saw Brinkmann in what was now a blood-soaked bathrobe. She yanked off her motorcycle helmet and threw it on the floor.

"Oh shit, oh shit" shouted Decker, as she ran towards a badly bleeding Brinkmann.

Brinkmann's eyes were glazed as Decker grabbed a hold of her and slapped her across the face.

"Don't you dare die on me Sergeant!" she shouted, "come on!"

Brinkmann's eyes partially opened as she grabbed hold of Decker's jacket.

"Took your sweet bloody time, didn't you?" she croaked.

WHEN THE DEPARTMENT 89 backup team arrived, it was headed up by Schmitz who raced into the building. Before he did so, he turned and pointed to the incoming police cars which were screeching to a halt.

"Stop them from coming up" ordered Schmitz to another operative, "this is our mess. We don't need the police putting their big feet in it. If necessary, call Busch and tell him to put his people on a leash."

Without waiting for a reply, Schmitz unholstered his gun and ran up the stairs, followed by department medical staff. He grimaced when he saw the dead bodies and the ruined door. He had a sudden sense of foreboding about Brinkmann. They had really done a number on her.

"Major!" he shouted, "Sergeant! One of you say something!"

"In here" shouted Decker.

Schmitz and the medics raced through to the bedroom to a scene of utter devastation. The overturned bed, the unconscious assailant on the floor, the blood, the bullet holes, the shattered windows. Schmitz was stunned, especially when he saw Decker holding an unmoving Brinkmann.

Schmitz's voice caught. "Is she...?"

"Dead?" said Decker, "no but she will be unless the medics get her to an operating room immediately. Our facility back at headquarters. Not a civilian hospital."

The medics nodded and immediately snapped into action, gently pushing Schmitz and Decker to one side.

"And him" snapped Decker viciously, kicking the ribs of the unconscious gunman, "he gets thrown into a cell in the Kreuzberg black site. No medical help. Leave him to suffer until we're ready for him."

Schmitz looked at an operative nearby. "You heard the Major. Nice and rough now. You saw what they did to Sergeant Brinkmann."

As they were dragging the unconscious man out of the room by the ankles, and Brinkmann strapped tightly into a stretcher, another operative appeared.

"Major, Captain" he said, "Chief Inspector Otto Busch is here. He is demanding to be allowed in."

Decker moved past and went downstairs, a frighteningly cold look on his face.

"Dear God" muttered Schmitz under his breath, "Busch has chosen an awful time to be an asshole."

BUSCH WAS outside in the street pacing back and

forth, a look of controlled fury on his face. When Brinkmann was brought out on a stretcher, he walked forward and studied her intently. When the unconscious gunman was dragged out, Busch erupted.

"He belongs to us!" he shouted, "hand him over!"

"Like hell we will" said Decker, striding outside, "he and his cronies attacked one of our own. We have jurisdiction. Don't like it? Take it up with the Chancellor's chief of staff. I guarantee though you won't get very far."

Busch pointed a finger at her. "This is the second time in eight hours you lot have caused havoc. First that truck outside Paderborn and now this. And I'm the one expected to clean up your mess."

"Get that finger out of my face before I break it" snapped Decker, "the suspect is coming with us, and your investigation, such as it was, is officially over. Now fuck off."

Before Busch could reply, Decker shoved him out of the way and walked to her motorcycle. Throwing on her helmet, she gunned the engine and took off for Department 89 headquarters. As she disappeared down the road, Schmitz came out of the building and shook his head at Busch.

"I don't know how my predecessor put up with this shit" said Busch.

Schmitz walked up close and got in Busch's face. "I'll tell you how. He learnt when to cut his losses, shut the hell up, and back off. Until you learn how to do that yourself, you're going to be a very deeply unhappy man, because nobody starts a fight with Major Decker and wins."

"We have laws in this country" said Busch irritably, "due process."

Schmitz snorted. "Chief Inspector, do yourself a favour. Learn the hierarchy and where you fit into it. The laws are there for ordinary criminals. Who we go after are not normal criminals, so we have extraordinary powers bestowed upon us by the Chancellor. Stop butting heads with us and realise what your predecessor realised. That you can occasionally take advantage of those powers if you need to circumvent the rules yourself."

"That will never happen" said Busch, forcefully.

"That's what Fischer initially said" said Schmitz, "and you'd be amazed how often he called asking for a favour. Don't burn your bridges with us Chief Inspector, because at the end of the day, when you're down and out, we'll still be standing."

CHAPTER FIVE

Tom Finn abandoned the car which had been stolen from a long-term car park, wiped down the interior, and then walked the extra mile to the safe house where the rest of his team were waiting. He was under strict orders not to approach the US embassy under any circumstances, as his mission was strictly off the books. So an apartment had been rented for them under a false identity.

Finn was furious. They had been given a golden opportunity to take out Penelope Brinkmann, and his so-called 'highly experienced field agents' had royally screwed up. Now Decker would know someone was coming after them. The element of surprise was lost and they had only been in the country for a few hours.

Brinkmann had been chosen as the first target because she was the easiest to find. Since she had originally been a member of the domestic intelligence service, the BfV, it had been easy for the CIA to contact one of their assets there to pull Brinkmann's human resources file and get her address.

Normally when someone joined Department 89, their file was transferred and placed under the highest security classification. But someone in either the BfV or Department 89 had made a colossal screw-up and forgot to purge her file from the BfV database. When confirmation came through that Brinkmann was still living at the same address, Finn saw the potential for a devastating first strike.

Except it didn't work out that way. That's what happens when you have an unknown team foisted upon you at the last moment. Finn pulled an encrypted phone out of his pocket, surreptitiously looked around to see if anyone was listening, and then dialled a private number at Langley.

"Yes?" said Lester after picking up on the first ring.

"It's me" said Finn, "the hit on Brinkmann went wrong."

A pause. "That's unfortunate Agent Finn. I thought you could handle something like this quite easily."

"Hey, don't blame this on me" hissed Finn into his phone, "you gave me a bunch of Goddamn interns, tea boys, and cleaning ladies. People I don't know and have never worked with. And you have the nerve to blame me for their incompetence?"

Lester sounded unimpressed with Finn's predicament. "How many did you lose?"

"Two dead, one captured."

"Captured?" said Lester, sharply, "Department 89 has one of them alive?"

"That's what 'one captured' meant the last time I checked" said Finn.

"That is unacceptable Agent Finn" said Lester, "Decker will break them and when she does, that agent will crack open like a tin of beans."

"You should have thought of that before giving me these idiots" said Finn gripping the phone tightly, "now we do things my way. Want to stop me? Come and get me. If you want this job done properly, stay out of my way." He hung up.

DEPARTMENT 89 HEADQUARTERS exploded into action when the ambulance carrying Brinkmann arrived. Not long behind the ambulance was Decker who had broken all speed records to catch up. As the ambulance screeched to a halt in the underground parking garage of their headquarters, Decker's motorbike could be heard roaring up behind them.

Department 89 had their own private clinic for injured operatives since, for obvious reasons, it was not safe to take them to a civilian hospital. Too many awkward questions would be asked, and a chance of the person's identity being leaked to the media.

So Decker had ordered the creation of their own clinic, equipped with state-of-the-art equipment, the best doctors in Europe, and the most highly skilled on-call surgeons available anywhere. Hans Unterwald, the chief of staff at the Chancellery, had paled when presented with the invoices for the construction work. But he was a pragmatic man and very quickly realised the need for Department 89 to have their staff medically treated at a secret secure location, away from prying eyes.

One of the surgeons hired by the government was suiting up in the operating room when Brinkmann was brought in. Doctor Henrik Weiland, a Dutch-German, whose ancestors fought the Nazis in the German and Dutch Resistance during World War II, blinked in shock as he took in the extent of the amount of blood covering Brinkmann's body.

"What was she attacked with?" he asked Decker who was waiting in the outer room.

"She was shot multiple times" replied Decker, shortly. "Don't let her die Doctor. I'm counting on you."

"I'll do my best" said Weiland, "but unlike most medical colleagues I know, I don't consider myself God. If she dies, she dies. But it won't be from lack of effort on my part."

He walked back into the operating room and closed the door where his colleagues were beginning to strip

Brinkmann and prep her for surgery. As the door closed, Decker frustratingly shouted obscenities at the top of her voice. She spun round and saw Schmitz standing there soberly looking at her.

"There's nothing we can do for her right now" he said eventually, "come on, Liebermann wants to see us. She's got something."

———

LIEBERMANN WAS busy tapping away at a keyboard when Decker and Schmitz walked in. Her small staff looked at Decker as she came through the door with "that look" on her face. The one everybody at headquarters knew only too well. It was the look that said that somebody was about to get seriously hurt. The look that made everyone instinctively turn away and avoid eye contact with her.

"Schmitz says you've got something" said Decker.

Liebermann looked as if she was about to cry. "How is Sergeant Brinkmann?"

"In surgery" said Decker abruptly, "what have you got?"

Liebermann snapped out of her grief and became businesslike again. Meanwhile, Schmitz rolled his eyes behind Decker's back at her total lack of sensitivity and tact.

"As you know, every senior member of Department

89 has a hidden security camera covering the front of their apartment building and across the street" said Liebermann, "I pulled the footage from Sergeant Brinkmann's camera a while ago and got pictures of the attackers."

She tapped a key on the keyboard and a high-definition movie file started, showing Finn's men crossing the street with guns by their side. They went into the building where the camera lost them.

"Well since all but one of them are dead, and the surviving asshole is in our custody, this doesn't really help us" commented Decker.

"Wait" said Schmitz softly, "she hasn't shown you the best part yet."

"As I said, the camera also covers the opposite end of the street" said Liebermann starting a new video file, "and we caught this gentleman crouching in the front passenger seat of a hire car".

The video started and it showed Finn in the front seat watching Brinkmann's building intently. The footage did not get a totally crystal clear image of him but he was recognisable enough if he was seen again. The video then showed him quickly driving away as Decker arrived at the building.

"Where was the car hired from?" asked Decker.

"Tegel airport" said Schmitz, "the car hire agency has a photocopy of the driver's licence by the person who hired the car. French licence and the identity is completely fake. We checked with our counterparts in Paris and the person on the licence is literally a ghost."

"CCTV footage inside the hire car agency?" asked Decker.

Liebermann tapped another key and another video came up. It showed a man in jeans and a hooded top taking great pains to keep his face away from the camera.

"He knew where the cameras were" said Liebermann, "so we don't have his face. Sorry."

"Has the car been returned to the agency?"

"Not yet" said Schmitz, "but we've put out a red flag on the number plate. Whenever it pops up, we'll be notified right away."

"That guy in the car" said Decker, "print out a photograph of him for me."

"What are you going to do with it?" asked Schmitz.

"Other than paste it into my 'assholes who need to be brutally murdered' scrapbook, I am going to show it to our prisoner and ask him not so nicely to identify his boss for us."

"And you know he's the boss...how?" said Schmitz.

"Because bosses don't march straight into buildings where they might get killed" said Decker, "instead they sit in the background and send in the cannon fodder. And the guy we captured has 'clueless donkey' written all over his face."

Decker walked out and Schmitz was about to follow, when Liebermann touched him on the arm.

"Captain?" she said softly, "There's something else you need to see. I don't know what to do with it and I didn't want to show it to Major Decker."

"What?"

Liebermann hesitated. "The camera outside Brinkmann's apartment caught Major Decker going in with Brinkmann during the early hours of the morning and not leaving until several hours later, shortly before the attack."

Schmitz stared at her, trying to digest what she was saying. He opened his mouth to speak several times but ended up saying nothing.

"I'm sure there is a very good explanation" he said, finally.

"Oh I'm sure" said Liebermann, "but I would be remiss if I didn't tell somebody, and given the circumstances, I'm sure as hell not going to raise it with Major Decker. I'm sure you will know if the issue needs to be addressed or not. I'm happy to delete the footage and forget all about it if you order me to."

Schmitz nodded. "Put the footage on a USB stick and have it sent to my office. On the quiet. Then purge it from your systems. Not a word to anyone else. Thank you Sergeant."

CHAPTER SIX

Finn debated long and hard about what to do with the rest of Lester's people, who were waiting for him back at the safe house. In his current mood, he was inclined to ditch the whole lot of them and recruit his own people. He certainly knew enough people who would more than adequately do the job required of them.

But he knew that his life would get a hundred times harder if Lester decided that Finn was a loose cannon and sent over another team to neutralise him. Although he was furious at the director, he had to keep him on his side. Fighting Department 89 was going to be hard enough. Having to simultaneously fight a CIA black-ops team assigned to eliminate him and tie up loose ends would make things absolutely impossible.

Finally he decided he would use the remaining five team members, but he would assign them grunt work.

They would be used to distract Department 89 by running interference. Meanwhile, Finn's handpicked people who he had known for years and worked with many times, would be doing the real work, taking out Decker and her senior officers.

Lester's people would be resentful and pissed, but quite frankly, Finn didn't give a damn. They were lucky that Finn didn't just shoot them all right now and be done with it.

He arrived back at the apartment and tapped the prearranged signal on the door. After a few moments, the door opened with the security chain attached and a face peeked out.

"It's me" growled Finn, "let me in."

The door was closed briefly while the chain was removed. Then the door opened completely and Finn marched in.

"Where are the others?" asked the agent who had opened the door and was now looking out into the hallway with a clueless look on his face.

"They won't be coming back" said Finn, taking off his jacket.

"What do you mean, they're not coming back?" said a black female agent named Thorne, whom Finn regarded as having a serious chip on her shoulder. He really wanted to punch her.

"Two are dead and one has been captured. It was a total fuck-up OK?" shouted Finn.

"One was captured?" said Thorne, "who?"

"Mitchell" said Finn, "Decker got him."

The agents looked shell-shocked. "And Brinkmann?"

"Badly wounded but alive" said Finn, "any coffee round here?"

"In the kitchen" said Thorne, "get it yourself. I'm not your fucking mother." She walked out onto the balcony and lit a cigarette.

Bitch, thought Finn, she really is going to get punched eventually.

"So what do we do now?" asked another agent.

"Now we bring in replacements for the dead agents" said Finn, "you all get your assignments, and we get revenge for this morning. But first we need to get the hell out of here. When Mitchell cracks - and he will - this place will be swarming with Krauts. We need to get to the backup location right now."

"Mitchell won't crack" said the other agent, pompously.

"Fine" said Finn, "then stay here and wait to be arrested or shot. I don't care. Personally I am moving to the backup location."

———

THE AGENT KNOWN as Mitchell had been transferred from the black site in Kreuzberg to Department 89 headquarters. He had been shackled by the hands and legs, headphones playing loud heavy metal music placed over his ears, and a stifling hot black hood pulled over his head. He was then unceremoniously dragged into an interrogation room where Decker and Schmitz were waiting.

The hood was pulled off his head, making him blink with disorientation. He staggered back slightly as the headphones were removed. But the shackles stayed on. He blinked furiously as he struggled to focus on his surroundings and his already low morale was made worse when he saw the two people staring at him with ill-disguised hostility.

Mitchell of course knew who Decker and Schmitz were. He had read their files extensively in preparation for the mission. So assessing his situation, he realised he was in extremely serious trouble. He also knew that the agency would disavow him and no help would be forthcoming from the embassy. He was on his own.

He was pushed down into a chair and cuffed to the metal table. He glanced at a dent in the table wondering whose face had been used to make it. He decided it was better not to know.

Schmitz got up and walked around to behind Mitchell. He always felt that standing behind someone was the best move psychologically as they never knew what you intended to do.

"My boss here has just called you a clueless donkey"

said Schmitz, "frankly that's an insult to donkeys. What do you think?"

Silence.

Schmitz squeezed Mitchell's head wound where Decker had whacked him with her pistol. Mitchell squeezed his eyes closed and stifled a silent scream.

"No?" said Schmitz, "nothing? Maybe we need to start removing your stitches one by one by ripping them out with a pair of pliers?"

Mitchell suddenly had an insatiable desire to laugh. He turned slightly and spat at Schmitz, which partly hit his expensive tie. Schmitz looked at the saliva silently, then started to remove his tie.

"If there's one thing I hate, it's people ruining my clothes" said Schmitz. He wrapped the tie around both hands then wrapped it around Mitchell's neck, strangling him.

Mitchell's eyes bulged with panic but the cuffs meant he couldn't move from his position. Schmitz was standing behind him, slowly increasing the pressure, and looking at Decker as if to say "say when". Finally Decker nodded and Schmitz pulled the tie off Mitchell's neck. The CIA agent slumped forward, gasping.

"You're....fucking....crazy" rasped Mitchell.

Schmitz looked at Decker. "You were right. Clueless donkey. American accent, which means we know now where he came from. Langley just can't get the staff these days."

Decker leaned back in her chair and studied Mitchell who was now silently cursing his slip-up. "Your prints are not in a computer, and we don't have your picture on record, which means you are not working out of the US Embassy in Berlin. So when did you enter the country?"

Silence.

"What was your mission?" pressed Decker, "exactly."

Silence.

Schmitz slammed Mitchell's head into the table, taking extra care to push his hand into Mitchell's head wound. Mitchell grimaced in pain.

"When we ask a question, you answer" said Schmitz, "we Germans are old-fashioned that way."

Mitchell laughed again. "I've been trained to with-stand extreme interrogation methods. You think this pussy-footing around is going to break me? You people are a fucking joke. Let me go now and I might forget to tell everyone how incompetent you are."

Decker stood up and removed her jacket, revealing tanned muscled arms. The tattoo of a snake could be seen protruding from the sleeve of her tight black T-shirt. She then pulled a gun from a holster in the small of her back.

"You and your goons shot one of my people today" said Decker calmly, "Sergeant Brinkmann is now fighting for her life in an operating room. That means your life is hanging extremely precariously by a thread. If she dies, so do you."

She pointed the gun at Mitchell's head. "Talk. Who

sent you? What was your mission? Where are the rest of your team?"

Mitchell looked at her. "You wouldn't dare. Kill me and you'll have nothing."

"Who said anything about killing you?" said Decker. She moved to the side of the table and fired one shot into Mitchell's right foot, shredding the sports shoe he was wearing and exploding the bone. Mitchell screamed and threw up all over the table. The cuffs held firm and made sure he couldn't move. Blood soon pooled on the floor around the ruined foot.

"Housekeeping" said Schmitz, "scumbag vomit and blood in aisle one."

The pain in his foot was agonisingly unbearable and Mitchell was sure he was going to pass out. His pale face was drenched in sweat.

"Don't make me repeat the questions" said Decker, pointing the gun at the other foot.

"CIA!" screamed Mitchell, "I'm CIA!"

"You don't say" said Schmitz sarcastically, "who sent you?"

"Seventh floor" he croaked, "Lester."

"Mission?" said Decker.

"To kill all of you sons-of-bitches" gasped Mitchell, the pain coursing through him in waves.

"Why?" said Decker.

Mitchell laughed maniacally, despite the overwhelming pain. "Well, if you really need to ask...."

Decker pointed the gun at Mitchell's knee-cap which cut short his laughing. "I do. Humour me."

"Trent" said Mitchell through gritted teeth, "we know what you did."

Schmitz glanced at Decker, who was looking dispassionately at Mitchell. So they know, she thought. She always knew it would come to this eventually. She just didn't think it would happen so soon.

"How did you find out?" said Decker.

Mitchell laughed maniacally. "You were photographed at the North Korea peace treaty along with Meyer. It doesn't take a rocket scientist to figure out the rest. It's the worst kept secret at Langley that Trent had your plane shot down."

"Who's your boss?" asked Decker, showing the print-out of Finn in the car outside Brinkmann's apartment.

Mitchell flinched and suddenly shut up, defiantly turning his head to the side. Decker didn't hesitate. She fired into the right knee-cap. Mitchell screamed even louder, the crippled leg jerking uncontrollably, his jeans now drenched in blood. He started crying and threw up again.

"Wow, the cleaners are going to have a fit when they see the state of this place" said Schmitz, casually chewing gum.

Decker swung the gun up and pressed it hard against Mitchell's head. "Last chance."

"Finn" screamed Mitchell, through tears and pain, "Tom Finn."

"Thank you" said Decker, "if you had only told me the first time I asked, you would still have your kneecap. You're now going to tell me the location of where your team is hiding. If you hesitate just once, I will kill you. Tell me what I want to know and I might consider letting you live."

Schmitz leaned forward with a notebook and pen in his hand. "address please."

CHAPTER SEVEN

Private Joseph Bigelow the Third was bored. He had joined the US Marine Corp to get out of Alabama, see some action and kill some Arabs. But instead, he found himself pulling night shift guard duty at the front gate of the US Embassy in Berlin.

He yawned as he scratched his butt. Another few hours and his shift would be finished. Then he would get some shut-eye. The thought of his bed made him happy. But those thoughts were interrupted by a black car with tinted windows which drove up the street slowly.

Bigelow tensed. Although this was not the Middle East, any US Embassy anywhere in the world was a terrorist target. So he eyed the car nervously, ready to draw his weapon if it looked as if the car's occupants were going to attack the embassy. He was damned if he was going to catch a bullet in goddamn Berlin. There were no medals and glory to be had in Germany of all places.

The car stopped and the back door opened. Bigelow was about to wet himself in fear. This was it, he thought. The embassy was about to be attacked.

He gripped his gun with sweaty palms and waited, willing his heart to stop pounding. He was not allowed to step outside the US Embassy with a loaded weapon unless he was convinced there was a valid and immediate threat to the Embassy. An open car door did not consti-tute a threat.

A large bulky sack was suddenly thrown out onto the road. Bigelow almost soiled himself. *A bomb!*

The door was then slammed shut and the car shot down the road and screeched around the corner. Bigelow watched the car go then turned his attention again to the sack which was lying in the road. It hadn't exploded yet, which made it a rather unusual bomb.

Bigelow was stunned when he heard moaning. Did the sack just *move?*

"Cover me" he shouted in a sudden burst of bravado to his equally stunned colleague. Bigelow lifted his gun, left the embassy grounds, and made his way over to the sack lying in the road. Attached to it was a piece of paper which read :

EXPRESS DELIVERY TO BERLIN CIA STATION CHIEF

FROM CIA DIRECTOR NORMAN LESTER & CIA AGENT TOM FINN.

Cautiously, Bigelow loosened the top of the sack and peered inside. What he found was a highly bloodied, badly injured, bound and gagged Agent Mitchell, staring wildly at him.

AT THE WHEEL of the car was Amsel, whose job it was to dump Mitchell at the embassy gates. After Mitchell had been dumped by his colleague in the back, Amsel took out his phone and dialled Decker, as he navigated the dark Berlin streets.

"Package delivered" said Amsel, "I still think we should have shot the son-of-a-bitch."

"No, no, this way is much better" said Decker, "remember what I said. This operation is likely off the books. By dumping him at the embassy, he is going to face seriously uncomfortable questions by the CIA station chief who won't know why his agent is in Berlin. When news gets back to Finn that his name was on the bag, he'll know his agent talked and that his operation is blown. When the CIA director finds out the agent was dumped outside the embassy in a bag with his and Finn's name on it, he'll know his golden boy royally screwed up."

"So we don't have to kill anyone" concluded Amsel, "we'll just sit back and let Lester do it for us."

"Exactly" said Decker, "welcome to the brave new world of outsourcing."

WHILE AMSEL WAS DUMPING the trash outside the US Embassy, a Department 89 team was preparing to raid the safe house address, provided by Mitchell.

Since it was likely that the identities of all senior department officers were compromised and known by the CIA team, operational command had to be handed off to people further down the food chain. People not likely to be immediately recognised by Finn and his team.

This is why Sergeant Kristof Ludwig found himself creeping up the stairs to the door of the apartment, followed closely by ten colleagues, one of whom held a metal battering ram to take down the door.

There were others watching the apartment from another angle, and Schmitz and Graf were watching the operation from a surveillance van in the adjoining street, courtesy of a video camera mounted on Ludwig's helmet.

All were heavily armed with machine guns, pistols in holsters, and grenades attached to their utility belts. They wore bullet-proof vests, helmets, and gas masks. They were a fearsome sight and the neighbours looked terrified as they were quietly shuffled out of the building. Ludwig and the others stood to one side as a colleague dressed as a postman came up to the door with an empty box and rapped on the door.

"Post!" he announced loudly.

"Like a covert CIA black-ops team is going to honestly believe somebody has sent them a care package" commented Graf.

After twenty seconds without receiving a reply, the agent moved deftly out of the way, and Ludwig signalled for the soldier with the battering ram to come forward and take the door down. Ludwig was glad. He hated it when they opened the door voluntarily and surrendered. It took the fun right out of the job.

One hefty swing was all it took to take the door right off its hinges. Stun grenades were immediately thrown in and the loud bang shook the building to its foundations. Liebermann had taken the regular stun grenades and amplified their power, making these ones a horrible and immensely traumatic experience for anyone not wearing a gas mask and ear plugs, as well as not closing their eyes at the moment of detonation.

The team swarmed in and methodically went from room to room, rifles raised, ready for any trouble. But it soon became apparent that there was nobody there. Ludwig talked into the microphone attached to the video camera mounted on his helmet, knowing Schmitz and Graf were listening.

"Place is empty Captain. The birds have flown the coop by the looks of it."

Moments later, Schmitz and Graf came sprinting into the apartment and took their own look around. Satisfied the place was indeed empty, Schmitz grunted.

"Well, we kind of knew that they would be gone" he said, "only rank amateurs would stick around, knowing their safe house would be blown eventually."

"Captain" shouted one of the other soldiers who was in the kitchen, "in here".

Schmitz, Graf, and Ludwig walked through to find the soldier pointing to a corner of the kitchen ceiling. Schmitz squinted and realised what the soldier had found.

It was a tiny video camera with a steadily blinking light.

Schmitz walked to the corner of the kitchen, tilted his head, and looked at the camera thoughtfully.

"Hello Agent Finn" he said in English, "I'm sure you're watching and listening. In case you're wondering, Agent GI Joe gave up all his secrets and we've dumped him at the US Embassy, addressed to you and Director Lester. Boy, you and that hapless agent of yours are going to have some awkward questions to answer when the CIA Station Chief in Berlin gets going on you both. And how will Lester react to that, I wonder?"

Many miles away, in a darkened room, Finn and the

others watched and listened to Schmitz. Finn was humiliated and furious. The others merely stared in disbelief.

"Oh and in case you're wondering" said Schmitz, "Sergeant Brinkmann is out of surgery and is expected to be fine. You idiots can't even kill someone without botching it up. Obviously Lester didn't send his best people, only the fuck-ups. Major Decker sends her regards and wants you to know that your lives can be measured in days and hours. None of you will leave this country alive. You don't go for one of our own and expect to live to talk about it."

Schmitz then yanked the camera down and threw it into a Faraday bag, cutting off the signal.

"Over and out, you bastards" he muttered.

IN THE DARKENED ROOM, miles away, Finn looked with a furious intensity at the screen which was now filled with white static. The others looked at him apprehensively but it was Thorne that broke the silence.

"Guess we've lost the element of surprise" she said sourly.

Finn turned his head slowly and looked at her with pure malice in his eyes.

"You think?" he snapped. "No shit Sherlock."

"So what now?" said another agent, Donaldson.

"Nothing changes" said Finn, checking his weapon,

"we have a mission to carry out and we're going to do it. We proceed to the next target."

"Even though they know we're coming and security will be tightened?" said Donaldson, his arms crossed.

Finn silently appraised him for a moment and then snorted in derision at what he saw as Donaldson's cowardice. "Nobody said this would be easy. If you want to drop out, I'll be happy to send you back to Washington DC."

Donaldson raised his hand in mock surrender. "I'm still in. I'm just playing Devil's Advocate, trying to make you see both sides."

Finn loudly snapped the gun magazine back into place and holstered the weapon. "Well, don't" he said, and walked out.

CHAPTER EIGHT

CIA Berlin Station Chief Charlie Drake was in the arms of a beautiful German woman when he got the call that ruined his evening. As he was giving the woman's breasts some serious attention, he could hear his phone buzzing. Determined to ignore it, he kept going but eventually he stopped and sighed.

"Sorry darling, I have to take this" he said, taking the phone out of his pocket.

Her eyes rolled. "Whatever. Your loss, not mine."

She swung her legs off the bed and got up as Drake picked up the call.

"Drake" he snapped, "this had better be good."

As he listened to the agitated voice of his deputy on the other end of the line, the colour in Drake's face drained.

"I'm on my way. Put him in a room and lock the goddamn door. Nobody talks to him till I get there."

FINN WASTED ABSOLUTELY no time in assigning the worst, most patently waste of time assignments he could think of to the remains of Lester's people.

It wasn't just that they were fuck-ups in his opinion. It was also that he didn't know them and he couldn't work with people he didn't know. For all he knew, one or all of them could be reporting back to Lester behind his back, providing 'alternative' update reports. Finn couldn't risk that. Not if the job was to be done to his standards and satisfaction. That meant Finn bringing in his own people. People he could trust. People with no ethics, morals, or qualms.

The people he was thinking of hiring would have stormed Brinkmann's place with flamethrowers. Not casually walked through the door with a target stuck to their heads.

So after putting some of Lester's people on following low-level German intelligence operatives, and others on building surveillance, Finn picked up his burner phone and started making recruitment calls.

"WHERE IS HE?" said Drake as he arrived in the CIA offices at the US embassy in Berlin.

"In interrogation room one" said Jane Gold, his deputy, "this is an unmitigated fuck-up and no mistake. The guy is not out of this embassy and he refuses to give his name. He is also severely injured. His foot is blown to pieces and so is one kneecap. Someone got very generous with their bullets."

"Pity they didn't use an extra one to kill him" said Drake, sourly. "So how do we know he is one of ours?"

Gold showed him the label which came with the bag carrying Mitchell, addressing him to Lester and Finn. "We also took his fingerprints and I sent them quietly to a contact in DC. His name is Neil Mitchell. He's a black-ops contractor for Langley."

Drake closed his eyes and swore to himself. "And who is this Tom Finn?"

"Still checking but if he officially doesn't exist, we are going to have problems finding out, without the seventh floor realising we're sniffing around."

"Or maybe our unofficial friend in interrogation room one will tell us" said Drake, "I can be very persuasive that way. If there is one thing I detest, it is unsanctioned operations on my turf."

"It will have been sanctioned by someone at Langley" pointed out Gold.

"I don't give a shit" shouted Drake, "Langley is not Berlin. I have to deal with the Germans and I can't do that with out-of-control fucking Clint Eastwood's running around. As station chief here, I have the absolute fucking right to demand that I be read into all local operations. I think we can assume they had something to do with the shooting of that intelligence operative this morning."

"Brinkmann?" said Gold, her eyebrow arched in surprise, "you think that was Mitchell and his partners-in-crime?"

"I'll bet a month's paycheck on it" said Drake, viciously, "come on, time to find out."

MITCHELL LAY in the interrogation room, in a hospital bed brought in especially for him. He was struggling to stay awake, having been heavily drugged with morphine to deal with the pain. Preliminary work had been done to stop the loss of blood and he had been given a blood transfusion.

But Drake had made it clear Mitchell was not going to properly go into surgery until he had given some answers. When the doctor had strongly protested, Drake had cut him off with "it's called leverage".

"It's called 'unethical'" retorted the doctor.

"Boo-hoo" said Drake, "call the Samaritans and let them know for all I care."

Now Mitchell squirmed in the bed as the last tendrils

of pain started to fade, thanks to the morphine. He shuddered at the thought of his ruined foot and knee. He would be a cripple for the rest of his life, thanks to that bitch Decker. And he didn't exactly have warm fuzzy thoughts for the CIA at that moment either, truth be told.

He was so wrapped up in his thoughts that he didn't hear the door opening, and someone walking up to the bed.

"Who are you?" whispered Mitchell, his eyes struggling to focus.

But the person didn't reply. Instead, several bullets were fired from a suppressed pistol into Mitchell's chest. He died instantly. His killer then calmly left the room and quietly closed the door.

———

DRAKE AND GOLD walked up to the door of the interrogation room. But before Drake turned the handle, he suddenly stopped and looked at Gold.

"Let me do the talking" he said.

Gold shrugged as Drake turned to the door again and strode in. He was about to begin his opening verbal salvo when the gruesome bloody sight of Mitchell lying dead in the bed met their eyes.

As Gold rushed into the corridor to hit the alarm, Drake stared with disbelief at Mitchell's corpse.

"What the hell?" he shouted eventually over the

noise of the klaxon alarm, "this is supposed to be a fucking secure facility! How could this happen?"

IT WAS that same evening in a quiet bar restaurant in Berlin when the first of Finn's preferred recruits arrived for duty.

Finn was sitting at the bar eating schnitzel and fries, and drinking a beer. At the same time, he had one eye on the front door, so when Louis Fawkes walked in, Finn watched him warily as he approached. Fawkes' reputation preceded him.

Finn was well acquainted with Fawkes. They had served together ever since they were both teenagers. The two had joined the Marine Corp together at the age of eighteen, and from there, they signed up for special forces together, and then the CIA.

But from there, their paths had diverged. Even though Finn was a deeply flawed agent, he still had the intelligence and good sense to make sure nobody could prove anything. Or he made sure he had high-ranking influential backers who could dig him out of any hole he dug for himself.

Fawkes on the other hand was not as clever and clear-sighted. He was quite bluntly a psychopath who didn't care what people thought of him. Therefore his CIA career was cut abruptly short when he was caught selling surplus Russian nuclear missiles and then murdering people who found out about it.

But before Fawkes could be brought up on charges, he fled for parts unknown. Finn always knew where he was however, and he owed Fawkes for saving his life in Panama. He also knew his psychopathic friend would help him get the job done, no matter what needed to be done.

"Thomas" said Fawkes, grinning his usual wolf-like grin, "as I live and breathe. I was wondering just yesterday how I was going to pay the rent this month, and here you are offering me work."

"Louis" said Finn, "a large part of me doubts you will ever have money issues. What we did in Panama probably set you up for life."

Fawkes merely grinned and took a French fry off Finn's plate.

"So what do I owe the pleasure?" said Fawkes munching, "what is the nature of this employment you're offering?"

"The usual" shrugged Finn.

"Death, destruction, suffering" monotoned Fawkes with delight, "right up my alley. When do we get started?"

"When the others get here."

"We will have company?" said Fawkes, "how delightful. How many and have I met them before?"

"Five more and no you haven't met them before" said

Finn, putting a large piece of schnitzel into his mouth, "but they have my personal backing so that should be good enough."

Fawkes considered this for a moment. "I guess. But remember what happens to anyone who gets in my way."

Finn suddenly lost his appetite and pushed away his plate. "Yeah I remember what happened in Panama."

"And where are the people who came with you from Washington?" said Fawkes, "don't tell me Lester sent you on your ownsome to deal with something this big?"

Finn smiled coldly. "They're about to get a big rude awakening. Don't worry, they will not be an issue for much longer."

THE REST of the team were at that moment in a new safe house awaiting the return of Finn. Little did they know that Finn had absolutely no intention of returning.

The black female agent, Thorne, who was nominally Finn's deputy on the mission, looked at her watch nervously and paced the bedroom. She hated crackerjack hotshot agents like Finn who had no discipline or respect for other colleagues. You could never rely on them in a tight situation.

Just like now for example. Where the hell was he?

Finn had given serious consideration to killing all of Lester's people but he had decided that he could sell the idea to Lester of them all being mysteriously captured while he was out on an assignment. That was why the front door of the apartment was suddenly blown off its hinges catapulting Thorne backwards against the wall. Stun grenades thrown by Department 89 forces into the hallway ensured resistance was quick and futile.

As the CIA agents lay on the floor stunned and retching, a gas mask-wearing Schmitz walked in and looked at them all.

"Delightful" he murmured and gestured to the squad leader to begin hauling them out one by one.

THE REST of Finn's team soon arrived. Bailey, Gardner, Dixon, Cassidy, and Abney. Fawkes alienated them right away by assigning them all nicknames and disparaging their experience.

Finn suddenly had second thoughts about hiring Fawkes but decided there was no time for civil war. With a look that silenced Fawkes, Finn started to explain the mission and what needed to be done. They would be paid out of a CIA secret slush fund and afterwards they would have to take new identities and retire. Did anyone want out?

No-one did. As Finn knew already, they were all psychopaths. Probably all heading straight to Hell. They probably wouldn't need the new identities in the end.

"I hate to state the obvious" said Bailey, "but if this group are outside the mainstream intelligence community here in Germany, we can't use our usual moles to provide us with information as to the identities of operatives or the location of their headquarters. So how do we find them?"

Finn looked approvingly at Bailey. "If we can't go to them, we'll force them to come to us."

CHAPTER NINE

The remaining members of Lester's agents who had been forced upon Finn were dragged out of a black van which had roared into the underground parking garage of Department 89. Covered in black hoods and bound with shackles, the stunned and frightened agents were roughly manhandled out of the vehicle and hauled into an elevator to the cells.

Schmitz high-fived the squad leader then made his way to his office. On the way, he had texted Decker and asked her to come to his office for a chat. Before the raid, he had had a chance to look at the CCTV footage of her going into Brinkmann's apartment during the night for what was plainly not business-related.

To say he was disturbed would be putting it mildly. But this was Decker and she wouldn't take very kindly to being embarrassed like this. So he had to be delicate about this and hope she didn't punch his lights out.

When he got to his office, he found her already waiting. She was sitting on Schmitz's office sofa, drinking very strong black coffee.

"So how did it go?" was her first words as she took another sip from her cup.

"Like a Swiss clock" said Schmitz, who made much of the fact that his maternal grandfather was Swiss, "they never knew what hit them."

"How the hell did we get them in the first place?" said Decker, looking suspicious.

"Anonymous phone call to emergency services" said Schmitz, "although if I had to wager a bet, I'd say it was Finn paying off his staff and terminating their services. The voice just gave an address and said 'tell Department 89 that's where the rest of the team is'. The mention of Department 89 sent so many red flags waving that I think the emergency operator is still traumatised."

"Lester is going to be pissed" said Decker.

"Like you give a damn" said Schmitz, who sat down behind his desk and opened his laptop.

"I get the feeling I wasn't called here to discuss your latest achievement" observed Decker, "spit it out."

Without replying, Schmitz put the USB stick containing the CCTV footage into the laptop, spun it round so Decker could see the screen, then started it. As Decker saw herself on the screen roughly pushing

Brinkmann up against her apartment wall outside, Decker's face paled. Schmitz suddenly wondered if he had just put his life on the line.

"Turn it off" she said with steel in her voice. Schmitz didn't need to be told twice, "where did you get it?"

"You really have to ask?" said Schmitz calmly.

"Fucking Liebermann. She's finished for this."

"For what?" exploded Schmitz, "imagine the situation you've put that poor woman in. She's scouring CCTV footage to find out who attacked Brinkmann and all she sees is you humping the victim up against a brick wall."

"Careful" growled Decker, "remember, I'm your superior officer."

"And you're also Brinkmann's" retorted Schmitz, "which begs the question of why you would be so monumentally fucking stupid as to do something like this. For a start, you know full well it's a court-martial offence, and secondly you knew damn well the cameras were there. It's almost as if you wanted to get caught."

As Decker slowly sat down on the sofa, Schmitz said "and for the record, if you retaliate against Liebermann, I will resign and make it clear to Unterwald why I am resigning. In *extremely* clear detail."

That earned a long glare from Decker but Schmitz suddenly felt emboldened. He didn't care anymore. He knew he had the upper hand here.

"Talk to me Major" he said softly, "what the hell were you thinking?"

"I wasn't" she said eventually, "you know how long it's been since I've had sex? Too long. For a long time, the job was a sex replacement, but I'm only human believe it or not. Suddenly I craved company and Brinkmann was available. I didn't pressure her. It was consensual. But I'm not stupid. I know you can end my career with that USB stick. So, the question is, what are you going to do now?"

Schmitz almost looked offended. He took out the USB stick, threw it to the floor and stomped on it till it was broken.

"The only copy" he said, "and for the record, there was never any intention to end your career. I just wanted to make you aware that you were caught. So don't do it again. I'll talk to Brinkmann when she wakes up and ensure she understands she needs to keep this to herself. Liebermann has already volunteered to have her entire memory wiped and her brain replaced."

Decker suddenly felt emotional. "What would I do without you?"

Schmitz shuddered. "God knows. It doesn't bear thinking about."

FINN and his new team watched as their next target left their government compound in the back of an armour-plated vehicle. They had decided the only way to get Department 89's immediate attention and force them out into the open was to hit a high-profile target. Someone whose kidnapping and death the German government could not ignore. Someone whose death they would feel duty-bound to retaliate against.

With another vehicle containing a protection detail in front of the government car, they quickly turned right into the main road and gradually picked up speed. The protection detail's car with its high-pitched siren ensured that traffic and pedestrians quickly got out of the way.

Since the rest of Lester's team were now off his hands, Finn was now feeling much more confident. His new team wouldn't hesitate to throw a little old lady under the bus if the mission called for it. In fact, when he described the mission to them, he could swear he could see them salivating at the thought of what they were being asked to do.

Now they were getting ready to strike a major blow against Meyer's government and Department 89. It would wipe the smug look off the faces of Decker and her people, and they wouldn't be so quick to think they had the upper hand anymore.

Finn's team was now split into two cars, and Finn absently touched the earpiece in his right ear as a small click could be heard, and a voice softly informed him the target's car was approaching.

"Do it" he said, while at the same time signalling to

the driver of his car. The vehicle eased into the road and edged behind the target's car. They were careful to keep to a reasonable speed to avoid bringing suspicion to themselves.

The car further on waited till the protection detail car in front of the target got closer. Then they shot out and the car screeched to a halt. Jumping out, Fawkes pulled out a bazooka, aimed it and fired with glee at the target's bodyguards. With a whistling screech, the missile shot out of the launcher and hit the protection detail's vehicle head on, causing it to erupt into a fireball, killing everyone inside instantly.

The driver inside the target's car, to his credit, reacted fast. He slammed the brakes on, and reversed the car causing it to go backwards down the road.

"We're under attack!" shouted another of the agents inside the car into his microphone, "I repeat, we are under attack. Request immediate heavily armed backup!"

Finn's car soon put a stop to any attempt at escape. Stopping the car suddenly and leaping out, Finn, Bailey, and Abney opened up with automatic weapons, taking out the tyres and punching huge dents in the bulletproof glass.

Finn knew they had to work fast. They were now on a clock. No doubt heavily armed reinforcements were already on their way and they had limited ammunition and weaponry. They couldn't win if they got themselves into a protracted gun battle.

Nodding to the others, he watched as they ran up to the car and attached plastic explosives to the locks of the rear doors. Within seconds, a loud boom blew the doors open and thick black smoke made the occupants wheeze and gasp as they staggered out of the car.

The bodyguards inside the car decided at that point that they had to fight as best as they could and hope reinforcements would show up in time. Firing their guns at their attackers, they succeeded in killing Abney. But the numbers were against them and eventually, despite their best efforts, they were all gunned down.

Finn sprinted up to the remaining figure, who had fallen out of the wrecked back door, wheezing and struggling to get on his feet. Finn grabbed him by the scruff of the neck and landed a solid punch on the jaw.

"Guten Morgen, Director Wagner" said Finn, "so nice to make your acquaintance at long last. Please, we have a car waiting."

Wagner was unceremoniously hauled to his feet, dragged to Finn's car, and flung through the open car door. All around them, the smell of burning and death filled the air. Civilians cowered behind street corners, some filming with their cameras, while sirens could be heard in the distance.

By the time backup government operatives arrived at the scene of the carnage, Wagner and his kidnappers were long gone.

DECKER WAS in her office studying a file when Schmitz walked in with a tight look of fury on his face.

"What?" said Decker, blankly.

Without replying, Schmitz picked up the TV remote control and turned it on to a German 24 hour cable news channel. Suddenly the screen was filled with the mobile phone footage of the attack and one tourist's footage of Director Wagner being hauled to his feet by Finn and bundled into another car.

Schmitz looked at Decker and stated the obvious. "They've got Wagner."

Decker sprung out of her chair and grabbed her jacket. "Come on."

"Where are we going?" asked Schmitz.

"The Chancellery. The CIA just declared outright war on us and I want Meyer's permission to declare war right back on them."

CHAPTER TEN

Tied tightly to a post with thick heavy ropes, Wagner's head was slumped slightly to the side. His wavy hair, normally white, was now matted with blood and sweat. It was running down his face, hindering his ability to see clearly. He blinked furiously trying to clear his vision, to no avail.

It didn't matter. The room he was in was dark and one eye was swollen shut due to the relentless brutal assault he had endured over the past several hours. He ran his tongue carefully along the inside of his closed mouth and felt several teeth either completely loose or moving about in his gums.

He knew in his heart that he was going to die here in this cold dark place, and this made him start thinking about his estranged wife, something he hadn't done for many years.

What would she say when the police came to tell her that her ex-husband was dead? He could imagine her stoic acceptance that the day had finally come, the day she told him would *inevitably* come, which was why she could no longer be with him. She couldn't wait at home every day as the dutiful wife, waiting for the knock on the door. She told him his job would ensure he would end up dead in a ditch somewhere.

"We all die eventually my dear" he had said, before walking out for what would be the final time.

Now it was going to happen. The thought of darkness enveloping him and an eternity of nothingness suddenly felt extremely appealing. He resolved to himself right there and then that he would give his kidnappers nothing at the end. They would be cheated of whatever information they wanted. He would not give them the satisfaction of seeing him crack and beg. He would also do whatever he could to hasten his end.

He was under no illusion as to the eventual outcome. There would be no rescue at the last minute, no reprieve from the cavalry. Nobody knew where they were and he couldn't hold out for much longer. But the thought of getting the final laugh made him smile, even though his body was shaking with intense pain.

Suddenly Wagner heard a scraping in the corner of the room and realised his attackers had been there all along watching him. Most of them stood in the darkness at the back but one of them, presumably the leader, stepped forward into the light.

"Find something amusing?" Finn asked softly, "I don't see much in your situation that bears laughing at."

Wagner opened his mouth and spat a broken tooth out.

"Tom Finn I presume. We've been here....what? Several hours?" he replied hoarsely, "and what have you accomplished in that time? You've beaten a helpless old man senseless. You must be really proud of yourself. Be sure to update your Twitter page and let everyone know about what a big boy you were today. Mummy will be proud."

He knew he was goading him which would only lead to more pain but he was past caring. *It will soon be over.*

"Helpless?" said Finn, an eyebrow raised, "that description hardly fits you. How many people have you killed with your bare hands in your career? Twenty? Thirty? More?"

"And you would be next if you had the guts to loosen my ropes and make it a fair fight. But no, you're too scared and so you had to tie me up and beat the shit out of me. Loosen the ropes and let's see how brave you really are."

Finn smiled and slowly clapped his hands in mock applause. "What a speech Director Wagner. Truly Oscar-worthy. Maybe they will remember you in the 'In Memoriam' section."

"I'm never going to tell you anything and I am not going to beg for my life" said Wagner, "so give it up and go home. You're an amateur desperately trying to be a professional. But you're just fucking useless."

Finn whipped out a handgun and pressed it hard against Wagner's forehead. The pressure added to the pain in his head but he didn't care. He closed his eyes and breathed deeply. But suddenly he opened his eyes and smiled at Finn.

"Actually, I do have something I want to say to you. Something really important. You ready to hear it?"

Finn's eyes narrowed suspiciously. "I can hardly wait."

Wagner started to laugh uncontrollably. "Major Decker is going to fucking torture you and murder you. Every last one of you. Then she'll go after your family, your school friends, nanny, wet nurse, and the first girl you jerked off over. She'll send you all straight to hell, where I'll be waiting to piss in your face."

With a howl of rage, Finn fired one shot into Wagner's head, and what was left of his head slumped to the side. A large amount of blood was on the floor behind him, courtesy of a large exit wound to the back of the head. As the last echoes of the shot faded away, an eerie silence descended over the room. Finn's hands were shaking from the adrenalin.

"Well, that's that then" commented Fawkes, "no coming back from a bang bang to the head".

Without replying, Finn walked over and put a sign around the remains of Wagner's neck. It merely said :

Payback for Trent, Major Decker

"Let's go" said Finn, walking away. He did not look back.

AS SOON AS they were safely away, Finn used a disposable phone to call the police and report Wagner's location.

The others couldn't understand why they would quickly give away his location. Why not make the government look for him themselves? Why not cause them hours and days of uncertainty?

But Finn was adamant that he wanted to move things along quickly. The sooner he was out of this damn country the better, and the only way to speed things up was to provoke Department 89 into a blind rage and make them lose their judgement. At least Finn was hoping this would be the case.

Due to his phone call, Wagner was found less than twenty minutes later by senior officers of the Federal police. They phoned Chief Inspector Busch, who took one disgusted look at the sign around Wagner's neck, whipped out his mobile phone from his pocket and dialled a number from memory. The phone was soon picked up at the other end.

"Hans Unterwald?" said Busch, "Chief Inspector Busch here. We've found Director Wagner. He's dead. You'd better inform Major Decker and get her down here."

When he hung up the phone, he looked at Wagner's body then cursed silently to himself. He knew right there and then that the body count had only just begun. The director of the internal intelligence service was dead. That could not go unanswered and unavenged. Decker would see to that.

———

LATER, when he was asked, Schmitz said that he had never seen Decker so shaken in all the time he had known her. When she had walked into the darkened warehouse where Wagner's cold body was still tied to the post, she took one look at his shattered head, read the sign around his neck, then promptly ran to the corner and threw up. When she was finished, she looked up, her face completely white.

Schmitz himself was stunned and could feel himself getting emotional, a lump forming in his throat. Wagner had always had their back, during the good times and the bad, and for him to have met his end this way, in a cold damp room, tortured and then shot.....Decker was right.

The CIA had just declared war on them. Nothing was going to be the same again. Even when this war had been won and settled, grudges would still be there.

Schmitz took out his phone and snapped a photo of Wagner. This earned him looks of disapproval from the police forensics people there but Schmitz didn't care. He texted the photo to Unterwald. When he put his phone away again, he looked at one of them.

"Untie him" said Schmitz, pointing to Wagner.

"Can't" said the forensics technician, abruptly, "crime scene. Can't disturb it."

Schmitz furiously grabbed the technician by the scruff of the neck and shouted at him. "Give him back his bloody dignity. Untie him or I'll do it."

Before the startled technician could respond, Decker walked past them with a knife in her hand and she cut the ropes herself. Wagner's corpse, free of the ropes, slumped to the side. The police howled in protest, but like Schmitz, Decker didn't care.

Schmitz's phone pinged with a return SMS message from Unterwald.

Orders from M. Do what you have to. Kill them all.

Decker looked at the message on Schmitz's phone and nodded to the door. "Let's go. We have a war to fight."

———

IN HIS DARKENED OFFICE, Unterwald looked at the photo of Wagner that Schmitz had sent him. Suddenly and without warning, he started shaking. Then he started crying.

Chancellor Meyer was not much better. When he had informed Meyer of Wagner's death, she had slowly slumped down in her seat with the look of a deer in the headlights. Fumbling papers on her desk, she eventually got up and paced about the office. Eventually she turned with wet eyes and looked at Unterwald.

"They all die" she said in a choked quiet voice, "Tell Decker that. Everyone connected to this dies, no matter how they are involved. No mercy."

Unterwald nodded silently and left the room to send the SMS reply to Schmitz. As he closed Meyer's door, he could hear her quietly sobbing.

As he now sat in his own office crying to himself and mourning the loss of his friend, Unterwald took out his phone and texted a SMS message to Norman Lester in Washington DC, along with the photo of Wagner.

You've declared war on us you son of a bitch. We have your team. Now Decker is coming after you.

He then threw the phone on his desk in a fit of rage.

It bounced off the surface and landed on the floor. Without bothering to pick it up, he snatched a bottle of Schnapps from the desk drawer, loosened his tie, and drank a generous mouthful straight from the bottle.

CHAPTER ELEVEN

Norman Lester was in a monotonous budget meeting when his phone pinged. When he saw the grisly photo and the message, the look on his face was scarlet and livid.

Finn had lost it this time. He had crossed the ultimate line. His brief was to take out Department 89 in a way that could be denied by Washington DC. He was *not* told to take out the director of Germany's internal intelligence service. Especially in front of tourists smartphone cameras. Germany was a NATO ally for Christ's sake.

What Finn had done was likely going to get the US Ambassador expelled from Germany and the embassy closed. Maybe even result in a declaration of war from Berlin. Expulsion from NATO. Christ, that didn't bear thinking about. Thank God the US wasn't a signatory to the International Criminal Court.

And the entire team was captured? It didn't take a genius to know Finn had gone off his medication and turned them all in.

He needed to cover his butt right now. He needed to start thinking about legal liability and exposure.

"Everybody out!" he snapped. His staff grabbed their files and scurried out. They had sensed the change in atmosphere and suddenly had pressing engagements elsewhere.

Lester picked up his desk phone and phoned Finn's mobile in Berlin. It went straight to voicemail. Cursing, he hung up without leaving a message. He stabbed a speed-dial number on the pad which connected him to the White House.

"I need an immediate appointment with the President. It's an emergency. Yes...of course right now. You think an emergency can wait till next week?"

PRESIDENT ROBERT GALWAY was sitting behind his desk in the Oval Office focusing on the documents in front of him. He sighed as he scanned and initialled each page with his pen. He stopped suddenly, removed his tortoiseshell glasses and began massaging the skin between his eyes. He hadn't had a whole night's sleep since his sudden ascent to the Oval Office.

The phone on his desk buzzed suddenly and Galway

jumped. Tightly squeezing his eyes closed, and fighting off the tiredness, he picked up the receiver and gingerly held it away from his ear. His secretary was renowned for speaking loudly.

"The German Chancellor Claudia Meyer is on the phone Mr President. She is requesting to speak with you."

Galway blinked. This was not protocol. All calls with foreign heads of state had to be pre-scheduled and go through the Secretary of State, or the White House Chief of Staff. A head of state could not just phone up the President of the United States directly.

Galway's secretary seemed to read his mind. "I told her chief of staff that there were procedures that had to be followed, but Mr Unterwald is a very rude man. He told me in rather unpleasant language what I could do with my procedures."

Galway rubbed his head even harder as the thought of his bed and a sleeping mask suddenly felt very appealing. "Fine, I'll take the call. Put it through."

"Yes Mr President."

A few seconds later, he could hear his secretary on the line again.

"Chancellor Meyer, Mr President."

"Madam Chancellor?" said Galway, "this is highly irregular. Calls should be coordinated...."

"Why did you do it?" interrupted Meyer harshly, "what did Klaus Wagner ever do to you?"

Galway stopped. This didn't sound good. "I don't have a clue what you're talking about."

"I hope you're lying because if you're telling the truth, you have a serious problem on your hands. My director of internal intelligence, Klaus Wagner, has been assassinated. And your CIA is responsible."

Galway breathed deeply and gripped the phone receiver. "That is an extremely serious allegation you're making, Madam Chancellor. I hope you have the evidence to back it up."

"Ask your CIA director if he did it" said Meyer sharply, "then get back to me. But I'm warning you now, if the German government does not receive a satisfactory reply from you by close of business today, we will consider the assassination of our intelligence director an act of war by the United States. And we will respond accordingly."

"Just wait one damn minute...." hissed Galway.

"And we want Agent Tom Finn of the Central Intelligence Agency handed over to the German government on a charge of murder. Your State Department will shortly receive the arrest warrant and extradition request."

Meyer hung up.

Galway sat stunned, listening to the buzzing of the disconnected phone line. As soon as he put the phone down again, it rang.

"Mr President?" said his secretary, "the CIA Director is here, requesting a meeting. He is not in the schedule."

"Oh is he really?" said Galway, "well, that's good as it saves me from having to summon him. Send him in please. I also want the Director of National Intelligence here right away."

"I believe he is here in the building Mr President. Meeting with the National Security Council."

"Fantastic. I also want him in my office right away. His other meeting can wait."

———

IN HINDSIGHT, Lester should have known that he was walking into a trap the moment he stepped into the Oval Office. Galway was in a foul mood but at the time, Lester was not duly concerned. Ever since Galway's sudden inauguration as President upon the death of his predecessor, Bill Trent, Lester had held Galway in contempt.

The feeling was mutual across most of the government and intelligence community. Galway had heard every insult imaginable and then some previously thought unimaginable. He had been labeled everything from a coward to a wimp to a waste of space. He was seemingly not fit to lick Trent's boots, never mind attempt to fill them. He was considered to be a temporary sufferance, a seat warmer for the last couple of years of Trent's term, before the party found someone more to their liking. Someone without a conscience, Galway's wife had said. Someone who eats babies instead of kissing them, like any good politician.

Since nobody had time for Galway, they had shown their contempt by delaying the news of Wagner's death. So when Meyer had called and given Meyer both barrels of her verbal shotgun, Galway had been caught totally off-guard and therefore humiliated. He now realised this and decided enough was enough. He had to assert his authority.

"Mr President" said Lester, a hint of contempt creeping into his voice, "thank you for fitting me into your very busy schedule."

To his surprise, the President did not immediately reply. He was reading a file and making copious notes in the margin.

"Mr President....." said Lester again, but he was swiftly silenced by Galway lifting a finger.

The only sound in the room was the steady ticking of the clock and the scratching of Galway's pen on the file. Lester sighed deeply and ostentatiously, making a not-too-subtle hint that he was finding Galway's theatrics tiring. Galway got the hint but kept ignoring his intelligence chief.

Finally there was another knock at the door and the Director of National Intelligence walked in. A grizzled 57 year old former army special forces Colonel and intelligence veteran, James Barton had served multiple presidents from both parties. He did not tolerate fools gladly and was one of the few people who actually sympathised with Galway's predicament. He had been told by an aide of Wagner's death but so far, he had not connected the incident to the CIA.

Barton also hated Lester's guts which made him one of Galway's most valuable allies. A sign of the deep animosity between the two Intelligence chiefs became immediately apparent when Lester shot an evil look at Barton and realised that he was suddenly out-numbered. His plan to talk down to Galway had just evaporated.

Galway threw down his pen and looked at the two men for a few seconds before finally speaking.

"Would either of you like to brief me on a matter of the most urgent national security? Is there anything I should know at this precise moment? Director Lester? Maybe you would like to go first?"

Christ, he knows, thought Lester. But he was beaten to the punch by Barton who relished the chance of sticking the knife into Lester.

"The director of the German internal intelligence service has been assassinated" said Barton, solemnly.

"Indeed" said Galway, "and can either of you explain how I only learned of this news when a furious German chancellor just called me and accused us of being responsible? Why didn't my own intelligence agencies rush to tell me?"

Barton flinched. "She is accusing us of murder?"

"Yes shocking isn't it?" said Galway, sarcastically, "that one of our longest and most reliable allies would accuse us of such a heinous crime. Wouldn't you agree, Director Lester?"

Lester didn't immediately reply. He was seething. Barton turned and looked at his colleague with the shock slowly registering on his face.

"What have you done, Lester?" he whispered. "Have you just started a war with Germany?"

Lester finally broke his silence but refused to make eye contact with Barton, instead staring straight ahead. "They've already declared war on us."

"Oh this will be interesting" said Galway sarcastically, "please do explain how you got to that conclusion?"

Lester briefly hesitated, then jumped in with both feet. "They assassinated Trent."

"Trent had a heart attack" snapped Barton, "we all know how far up his ass you were, but there's no need to project your inconsolable grief onto other people."

"It wasn't a heart attack" retorted Lester, "it was an assassination."

Before Barton could respond, Galway lifted a finger to silence him. "And why would Germany want to assassinate our president and risk war with us?"

Lester was suddenly reticent. His loyalty to his old boss made him reluctant to drop him in it. As he was fond of saying, Trent was a son of a bitch, but he was *his* son of a bitch.

Barton was fast running out of patience. "The President asked you a question."

"President Trent learned that a German intelligence team was being infiltrated into North Korea" said Lester uncomfortably, "he told Chairman Kim through backchannels and Kim had the plane shot down."

The shock in the room was palpable. "And you knew this?" said Barton. Galway was sitting behind his desk, his face in his hands.

"I didn't suggest it if that's what you're implying" said Lester stiffly, "on that score Trent was freelancing. But I learned of it after the fact."

"And said nothing" said Galway quietly.

"Who to?" snapped Lester, "you? Bill Trent was the President of the United States and my loyalty was to him."

"Your loyalty is to this country Director Lester" said Galway, leaning back in his chair, "you had a duty to report the President to the relevant Congressional Oversight Committee. But you didn't."

"I was loyal" growled Lester.

"But not to this country nor to me" said Galway, "and I can't have that. You have also made yourself complicit in Trent's crime by shielding him. Therefore I suggest you get an extremely good criminal defence lawyer because you will need one when the Justice Department is finished with you."

"You want my resignation?" said Lester.

"What? To spend more time with your family?" said Galway sarcastically, "no, you're fired. Now tell Director Barton how to rein in this rogue team you sent to Berlin or I swear to God you'll wish you had never been born. I am sick and tired of people undermining me and disrespecting me. Today it stops. Tell us how to stop this team of yours and it will be regarded favourably by the Attorney-General. I'll see to it."

Lester burned with humiliation at his sudden firing and what was to come. But he knew that unless he started racking up brownie points, he was headed to prison.

"I don't know" said Lester finally, "they are not operating out of the Embassy for obvious reasons. Finn betrayed his entire team bar three to Department 89 and he is now out in the wild not answering his phone."

"What do you mean 'bar three'"? asked Barton, the contempt dripping from his voice.

"Two were killed, one captured" said Lester, "they tried to kill a Department 89 operative and it failed badly. The captured one was tortured and dumped alive outside the Embassy addressed to Finn and I. But before the Station Chief could question the agent, the agent was murdered inside the Embassy."

"By who?" said Galway, looking shocked.

Lester's face was impassive. "Enquiries are ongoing."

Barton barked out a short laugh. "This is a comical farce and no mistake. Whoever did it will have long covered their tracks."

"Educate me on this Department 89 again" said Galway, "I got the highlights when I was inaugurated. Now give me everything."

Which Lester and Barton proceeded to do. By the end, Galway was thoughtful.

"And how did they allegedly assassinate President Trent?"

"We suspect poison" said Lester, "which made us believe it was a heart attack. The fact Major Decker was in the room at the time convinced us she was not there for a social call."

"Mr President...." began Barton.

"Wait" said Galway, picking up his phone and calling his secretary, "get me Chancellor Meyer back on the phone. Thank you."

"What are you going to say?" asked Lester as Galway put the phone back down.

"Wait and find out. But during the call, you will both keep quiet unless I specifically instruct you to speak. Understood?"

Before either man could reply, the phone buzzed again and Galway picked up.

"Chancellor Meyer, Mr President."

"Thank you. And while I am talking to her, please ask the Secretary of State and the Secretary of Defence to come and see me please."

"Yes Mr President".

"Chancellor Meyer?" said Galway when he was

connected. He covertly put the call on speaker so the others could hear.

"President Galway" said Meyer, coldly. "I hope you have good news for me."

"I have a question first."

"Go on."

"Why did you assassinate President Trent?"

A moment's silence which spoke volumes. "I don't know what you're talking about, and I resent the accusation. You can't prove it either."

"So you deny it?" said Galway, "oh well, I can always order President Trent's exhumation and an autopsy ordered. A more extensive one that will look for overlooked *toxins*."

"Go ahead" said Meyer, although she was pissed off that the shoe was now on the other foot, "you are aware that Trent betrayed my intelligence team to the North Koreans?"

"You can't prove it" echoed Galway, "and if indeed for the sake of argument you *did* assassinate Trent, then killing your intelligence director could be seen as...getting even?"

Barton looked at his boss in a mixture of shock and pride. Even Lester was reassessing his opinion of the President. Galway had suddenly grown a set of balls.

"Let's not deal with what we cannot prove" said Meyer, "The fact remains that one of your agents committed a cold-blooded murder on German soil. That is provable and beyond dispute. We have him on video footage committing the act. We want him for prosecution, and anyone working with him."

Galway took a deep breath. "That will not happen under any circumstances. Agent Tom Finn is our dirty laundry. We will take care of it."

"No way" snapped Meyer, "give him to us or we will sever diplomatic relations with the United States. And I'll be sure to tell cable news why I did it."

"And we will tell the media about President Trent's assassination, and Major Sophie Decker and Department 89's involvement. Oh yes, Chancellor Meyer, I am well aware of your little personal hit squad. We have photographic proof Decker was in the room when President Trent died. How would CNN react to that I wonder?"

"Stick to what you're good at" said Meyer, "and threatening people is not one of them. Now do we get Finn or not?"

"No" said Galway, "I think you have more to lose than I do, with assassinating our president....."

"I told you...."

"Therefore I am calling your bluff on this one Madam Chancellor" said Galway before hanging up abruptly.

"You're playing with fire Mr President" said Barton quietly.

Galway was spared from replying by the phone buzzing again.

"The Secretaries of State and Defence are here Mr President" said his secretary.

"Thank you. Send them in" said Galway. When he hung up, he looked at Lester.

"Get the hell out of here. I never want to see you again. You'll be hearing from the Attorney-General very soon. That I guarantee."

CHAPTER TWELVE

Meyer sat in shock behind her desk. She thought she had had the upper hand, but somehow they knew about Trent. For the first time in his life, Galway had grown up from a small boy into a man.

His timing is impeccable, she thought bitterly.

She looked across at Decker who was sitting opposite her. Decker had not reacted during the entire phone call and she now seemed to be waiting for a cue from Meyer.

"What do you think?" said Meyer.

"Galway will never give up Finn and the others" said Decker, "the CIA would rebel if he did. They already think he's pathetic. Although you have to admire his balls threatening you like that. Remind me never to play poker with him."

Meyer nodded. She knew Decker was right. She drummed her fingers on the table.

"Do what needs to be done" said Meyer, "you have full authority."

"Even if it means waging war against the United States?"

Meyer didn't reply immediately. Eventually she said "try not to let it get that far."

FINN and his team decided to follow up on the momentum of Klaus Wagner's assassination by hitting all known German Intelligence and political targets. They knew that eventually Department 89 would have to come out into the open and respond. Meyer's credibility and authority would depend on her putting down the attacks quickly and decisively.

The first to get hit were two off-duty intelligence officers standing in a bakery waiting to be served. Fawkes and Bailey walked in, fired point-blank shots into the backs of the agents heads and then walked out again to the sounds of screams from the customers.

Cassidy and Abney were waiting in the getaway car and Bailey frantically got in. Fawkes on the other hand coolly shot a bystander who had decided to play hero and then casually got into the car, the others furious at his recklessness.

Gardner and Dixon meanwhile were going after a high-profile Bundestag politician and former cabinet minister who was giving a speech in Berlin. They decided shooting him was not spectacular enough, so they lobbed several grenades into a hall where the politician was speaking, and thirty-five people were sitting listening to him. Gardner heard someone shout "GRENADE!" before a loud boom, followed by screaming, filled the air.

The presence of a former cabinet minister at the event meant there was also a police security presence. As Gardner and Dixon came running out of the building, they were intercepted by undercover police who came running towards them with guns drawn.

"*Halt!*" shouted one of them, "put your guns down."

Gardner and Dixon had no intention of giving up. Dixon swung up his gun to fire but the police officer was faster. He fired a shot into Dixon's chest, centre-mass, which shattered two ribs and ruptured an artery. As Dixon hit the ground hard, bleeding heavily, Gardner calmly dropped to his knees and fired one shot back hitting the officer in the throat.

The other officer saw his colleague die and decide to fall back and wait for reinforcements. He ducked behind a pillar as Gardner fired a volley of bullets in his direction. All missed.

By this point, all hell had well and truly broken loose. The plan was for Gardner and Dixon to get the metro to a pre-arranged location where they would be picked up. But the chances of that now were virtually non-existent.

The assassination of a former government cabinet minister and a police officer meant that everything would now be on lockdown - including all transport networks. And Dixon was seriously wounded, perhaps mortally.

Gardner knew what had to be done. Under opposite circumstances, Dixon would have done the same to him. After muttering a quick prayer, he shot Dixon twice in the chest. Dixon's body convulsed, then went still forever.

Reloading his weapon, he fired several shots in the direction of the police officer to persuade him to stay behind the pillar. Gardner cursed. The officer had seen Gardner's face and could identify him. But he was now running against the clock and he didn't have time to eliminate witnesses.

With one regretful look back at Dixon's corpse, Gardner ran in the other direction, determined to get as far away as possible. The blaring sound of approaching police sirens hastened his escape.

GARDNER DIDN'T ACTUALLY GO VERY FAR. He went around the corner, put on a disguise, changed his jacket, and waited. The whole point of what they had just done was to see if Department 89 responded to the incident. How could they know if he didn't stick around to find out?

The others, when they hit the bakery, were supposed to wait around too. But then Fawkes had to go and kill that civilian, and Finn had decided that it was too hot for them to hang around. Especially since Fawkes had shown his face to a dozen witnesses who were now busy telling the German police what they had seen.

Once Gardner was sure his disguise was as good as it could be, he ordered a coffee at a cafe, waited in the window seat and willed his adrenalin-pumping body to calm down. Nobody looked at him because they were too focused on the rising plume of smoke the next street over.

Little did they know that one of the men responsible was now sitting next to them drinking coffee and trying to act normally.

DECKER AND AMSEL were soon on the scene of the assassination of the politician. Schmitz and Graf were at the bakery. But a politician meant that Decker, as commanding officer of Department 89, instantly got the case.

As Decker got out of the armoured government car that Meyer had insisted all senior Department 89 operatives use for the time being, she was met by Chief Inspector Otto Busch, who uncharacteristically looked sombre and meek. He wasted no time in telling them why.

"I got a call from Chancellor Meyer's chief of staff, Hans Unterwald. I was very quickly put in my place. Seems my entire purpose in life is to follow behind you and clean up your messes."

"A very honourable occupation" said Decker, which earned a look of anger from Busch. But before Busch could reply, Amsel pushed Decker ahead and looked diplomatically at Busch.

"We appreciate all you do Chief Inspector" said Amsel, before continuing to push Decker towards the crime scene tape.

"Why do you have to antagonise him like that Major?" said Amsel, shaking his head.

"Because he's an ass" replied Decker, flashing his badge to the police officer on duty.

The place where the dead police officer and Dixon lay had been covered by a huge tent and was now crawling with white-suited forensics officers. Decker walked over and looked at the police officer who lay on the ground with a single wound to the throat. His eyes were slightly open as if he was surprised by what had happened. There was very little blood.

By comparison, Dixon was a mess. He was soaked with blood and it was clear he had taken several rounds to the chest. Amsel took a picture of him with his smartphone and sent it to Liebermann with instructions to get him identified through facial recognition.

But it was when they walked into the ruined hallway

where the politician and twenty-two of the thirty-five members of the audience lay dead that they got a shock. Not only because of the carnage but because Peter Humphries, British MI6 Station Chief for Berlin, was there. He was dressed in a duffle coat and floppy hat, making it look as if he was auditioning for Paddington Bear.

"Mr Humphries" said Decker, "why are you here? What interest does the British government have in the assassination of former minister Lesch?"

"Oh he usually revealed something of interest in his speeches, given that he worked in the defence ministry not too long ago. And his coffee and cakes afterwards were superb."

"Are you sure there's not another reason why you're here?" said Amsel.

Humphries looked at him with bemusement. "I don't think I've had the pleasure. You are?"

"Lieutenant Amsel."

"Well Lieutenant, all I can tell you is that I simply adored hearing about Lesch's opinions on NATO and the former Warsaw Pact, and the coffee....."

"Yes, you told us. Superb" said Amsel, clearly not believing a word of it.

"How did you survive the attack if you were listening to his speech?" asked Decker.

"Ah well, I was running late and missed the speech.

Traffic in Berlin is terrible. Thank God I did, otherwise I would be barbecued meat by now."

"What happened here exactly?" said Amsel.

"I think it's obvious what happened" said Humphries, "A big boom and everybody died."

Decker started to get irritated. "And the cause of this big boom?"

"Oh, right. Fragmentation grenade. Three of them. Tossed in by two individuals, one of whom is outside dead on the pavement. The other killed his partner when it was obvious the one outside was going to expire, then number two scarpered."

"Meyer is going to hit the roof" said Decker, "she was close to Lesch. He was her favourite defence minister."

"Until he was caught doing insider trading with defence stocks" said Humphries, "then he was not quite the favourite anymore."

Amsel's phone rang and he picked up. It was Liebermann. Amsel politely ignored Humphries' inquisitive looks and walked away. Decker took the opportunity to walk up and look Humphries in the eye.

"Anytime you want to abandon that chicken-shit story about listening to speeches and drinking superb coffee, let me know. Then you can tell me why you were really here. In the meantime, have a nice day."

As Decker walked away, the look on Humphries face turned cold. He took his mobile out of his pocket, dialled a number from memory and waited.

"It's me" he said when the other person picked up. "Lesch is dead and Decker the bloodhound is already seeing through my bullshit. We are going to have another one of those irritating Sophie problems again."

WHEN DECKER GOT OUTSIDE, Amsel was waiting for her.

"That was Liebermann. She's identified the dead man. He's......"

Suddenly a high-powered sniper rifle cracked and a bullet came whizzing towards Amsel and Decker. The bullet hit Amsel in the shoulder and shattered the bone. Decker grabbed a violently shaking Amsel and pushed him behind a wall. A wild-eyed Amsel was frantically clutching his shoulder and going into shock from blood loss.

There were no more gunshots so the police in the street outside had no clue where the gunman was. They were surrounded by tall buildings, any one of which could be concealing Tom Finn, who was now rapidly packing up his rifle and picking up his casings. Then he crawled away to make his rendezvous with Gardner and the others who were currently driving at top speed to pick them up.

"Where's that bloody gunman?" yelled Decker. By now, Humphries had also ran outside and was crouching beside Decker and a barely conscious Amsel who was futilely clutching his wound to stem the bleeding. Decker took off her jacket and pressed it against the wound, causing Amsel to scream from the pain.

"Stop being a cry baby" she snapped, getting her phone out with her other hand. She called ahead to headquarters, informing them of Amsel's injuries and to get Henrik Weiland, the on-call surgeon back in again.

As Amsel was bundled into an ambulance, Humphries looked at Decker.

"Do you get the feeling Lesch was the bait and you walked right into the trap?"

Decker looked at him. "Yes, but I am fed up being the mouse chasing the cheese. From now on, I will be the hunter, not the hunted."

"Which is precisely what these people want."

"You know about them don't you?" said Decker angrily.

"We hear things every now and then. But if you are asking where Tom Finn and his team are right now, we are as much in the dark as you are. If that changes, you will be my first call."

"I'd better be" said Decker, "because when my staff get picked off like targets at a fairground, I tend to take it very personally. Especially if I learn people are withholding vital information that I need. Keep in touch Humphries."

CHAPTER THIRTEEN

As Decker got back into the government car, her phone rang. It was Meyer.

"I heard about Martin Lesch" she said, "a good man. He didn't deserve what happened to him. By rights, he should have been my successor someday."

"I'm sorry, Madam Chancellor" said Decker, "Amsel got an identification from Liebermann of one of the attackers here before he was shot. I will find out who did this and deal with them."

"To that end, I have made a decision" said Meyer, "due to the death of Director Wagner, I am appointing you acting director of the internal intelligence service. Purely for the duration of this crisis. You will remain working out of Department 89, but this appointment will provide you with extra manpower for whatever purposes you deem necessary."

"And what about the deputy director?" said Decker.

"He will be your deputy" said Meyer, "if he has a problem with that, then tough."

"Thank you for your confidence Madam Chancellor. In the meantime, I have recommendations."

"I'm listening."

"Close the US Embassy and expel the ambassador and his staff. It's time we started making waves."

"The media will demand to know why" said Meyer.

"Screw the media. The official reason is Wagner's murder and the suspicion that the US was involved. If Galway accuses of you of Trent's assassination, deny it and keep denying it. They can't prove a damn thing. That toxin is untraceable, even in an autopsy. I made sure of that. Keep them on the defensive."

"People might consider the closure of the US Embassy a complete over-reaction" said Meyer.

"I have two badly wounded agents who may never work again, who would strongly disagree with you Ma'am" said Decker, who then hung up.

MEYER SAT and listened to the disconnected line tone. She thought about what Decker had just said. Unterwald was sitting on the couch, his arms folded, waiting.

"You heard her" said Meyer, "this has gone far

enough. Do it. The Foreign Minister is to designate everyone persona non-grata."

Unterwald nodded, got up and left the office.

AS DECKER WAS ABOUT to start the car engine, there was a rap on the window. It was Busch. Decker swore silently to herself. The last thing she needed was a rant from him. She buzzed the window down and waited for the rant - but it never came.

"There's someone here who claims to be the CIA station chief in Berlin" said Busch, "name of Charlie Drake. You know him?"

"Know *of* him" said Decker, astonished, "not like him to crawl out of his cave. Where is he?"

"Other side of the square."

"I'll get in the back of this car. You bring him over and tell him to take my front driver's seat. You guys watch the car and if there are any signs of trouble, get your asses over here. I trust Drake as much as I trust a cobra snake."

FIVE MINUTES LATER, the driver's door opened and Drake got in. He stiffened as Decker pushed a suppressed pistol into the back of his head. Then he relaxed and laughed.

"Major Decker, please. Even you wouldn't be so foolish as to blow my brains out over a car windshield in the middle of Berlin."

"I wouldn't be too sure about that" said Decker, "I've had a really bad week so far. Two of my agents have been badly wounded by CIA agents. I could do anything in the heat of the moment. I have to say Drake, I admire you coming over here in broad daylight to talk to me. Keep your hands on the steering wheel where I can see them. Are you carrying a weapon?"

"Nope."

"Then you're more stupid than you look."

"Hey I come in peace."

"Says the CIA station chief, while a rogue CIA black-ops team is running around Berlin killing high-profile politicians and intelligence operatives."

"That's right" snapped Drake, "that's the word of the day. *Rogue.* As in 'out of control, unable to be stopped.....'"

"I'm well aware of what it means" said Decker, "why are you here?"

Drake breathed deeply. "I was not told in advance of this team, therefore I did not sanction it. It was all Lester's doing. Lester has been fired by the way by Galway for concealing what Trent did to your plane."

"Tell somebody who gives a damn."

"Look, I am as furious as you are. I deeply respected Klaus Wagner and chaos like this does not do my reputation any good. It's in my best interests to have a calm peaceful environment where everyone joins hands and sings Kumbaya. But this...who benefits from this? Not us, not you, not your boss."

"And Galway? He can't order the team back?"

"Galway?" said Drake, barking out a laugh, "you're taking the piss aren't you? Galway couldn't fight his way out of a paper bag. Most of the US intelligence community is already looking ahead to the next administration. Besides, Lester has lost contact with his team. You can't order back people if you don't know where they are."

Decker got in close and pushed the barrel of her gun against Drake's head again, making him squirm. "What are you proposing? Because I have just recommended to the Chancellor that she close your embassy and turf you all out."

Drake turned slowly and looked at Decker. "That would be a mistake. Wars have started after less than this."

"Give us an alternative then" said Decker, "and eyes front. Don't look at me again."

"As a sign of good faith, we work together to end this" said Drake through gritted teeth, "the full resources of Berlin CIA station along with Department 89. I've spoken to the President and he has authorised it."

"Actually it would be the entire internal intelligence

department" said Decker, "Meyer just gave me Wagner's job on an acting basis. Not sure if that was a good idea but hey-ho, nothing ventured, nothing gained."

"You've been given the BfV?" said Drake, shocked, "not sure whether to congratulate you or run. But if Meyer is about to shut down the embassy, there goes Berlin CIA station. So I guess the proposal is moot. Great, thanks a lot."

Decker put the gun down and flipped the safety catch on. "They can only deport you if they can catch you. Stay away from the embassy and you'll be fine. I may be getting stupid in my old age but I have decided to trust you. But if you betray us in any way, I will kill you all and put you in a shallow grave. Do you understand me?"

"Absolutely. I don't doubt you for a second."

"Good" said Decker, "then we have an understanding. Can you get anyone else from the embassy to join you on this heroic but pointless quest?"

"Jane Gold, my deputy" said Drake immediately, "I'm going to reach into my pocket now to call her. For Christ's sake, don't shoot me."

"How's your agent by the way?" said Decker, "the one we dumped outside your front door?"

"That was you" said Drake sullenly, "I should have known it. He's dead."

Decker's eyes narrowed. "Oh come on, we didn't hurt him that badly."

"No but the person who put several rounds in his chest before I could question him did."

"From inside the embassy? Then under the circumstances, maybe it isn't wise to bring anyone else in. Maybe it isn't wise to trust you at all" commented Decker.

"Hey, I trust Gold completely" said Drake, dialling a number, "Gold? It's me, don't ask me any questions. Just get the hell out of the embassy right now. Walk out and don't look back. Take the back door and tell nobody where you're going. I'll meet you at our emergency meeting place."

"You mean platform one at the train station?" said Decker.

Drake looked startled. "You know our freaking emergency meeting place? Of course you do. Gold, get to the Bahnhof right now. I'll explain everything when I see you."

CHAPTER FOURTEEN

It was around the same time that the US Ambassador to Germany, Daniel Stokes, was summoned into the office of the German Foreign Minister, Lukas Hirsch, and informed that he and his staff had forty-eight hours to leave the country. When a deeply shocked Stokes asked for a reason, he was told it was in retaliation for the CIA assassination of Klaus Wagner.

Stokes, to his credit, didn't try to deny it. He had been briefed by Drake about the black ops team and obviously he knew about Mitchell being murdered in the embassy. The firing and imminent indictment of Norman Lester was exploding all over Washington DC and cable news, as it had leaked out that Langley was responsible for the murder of the intelligence director of a friendly country.

So in a way, Stokes had been expecting this moment.

He had been in the diplomatic service for too long to know that you didn't give a friendly nation a black eye like that and expect to walk away from it. So he stood up without saying anything more, formally shook Hirsch's hand, and pledged to be gone within the forty-eight hour deadline. Hirsch merely nodded and indicated the ambassador should now leave.

As he left in his diplomatic car, Stokes called his deputy ambassador.

"We've just been PNG'd. Start shredding the documents and pack everything up. Confine the staff to the embassy and tell them to start packing their bags. We're out of here."

DECKER WAITED until Drake was on the phone and out of earshot before calling Liebermann. She found out what Liebermann had told Amsel a short while earlier.

"Thanks Liebermann" said Decker abruptly, and hung up. She was still pissed with her for running to Schmitz about her personal life. She was in no mood to chat.

When Drake came back over, Decker looked at him.

"Frank Dixon" she said.

"Who?"

"Frank Dixon" she repeated. "We just got an ID on the guy lying on the ground there."

Drake's eyes flashed. "If he is CIA and off the books, how did you get his name so fast?"

The fact that Berlin and other major German cities now had security cameras on every street corner was classified at the highest security levels. There was no way she was going to tell Drake about it.

"We have our sources and methods" was all she would say.

Drake grunted. "Sources and methods, eh? Well I guess I would say the same if the roles were reversed. Frank Dixon....well my deputy has her 'sources and methods' as you say, back in DC. When we meet up with her, she can call her source and see who Frank Dixon really is. By the way, that was the ambassador on the phone. Gotta hand it to your chancellor. She moves fast. She just *persona non grata*'d all of the embassy staff and given them two days to leave the country."

"And what were your orders exactly from the ambassador?"

"To pack up and leave. Guess I will have to suffer selective hearing and ignore that order though. Got some rogue operatives to take down."

"This could mean the end of your career, Drake."

"Decker, I've been in the CIA now for close to sixteen years. And not once in those sixteen years have I ever been so disrespected and pissed on by Langley. As station chief, I was entitled to be read into that operation, but instead they treated my staff and I like we were irrelevant and untrustworthy. So fuck 'em. Time to take out the trash."

"So let's go. Your deputy will be waiting at the Bahnhof. Let's not freak her out by being late."

As Decker and Drake got into the car and drove away, Humphries stepped out from behind a pillar where he had been watching the two interact. He got his phone out again and called the same number.

"Me again. Seems Decker and Drake have teamed up like Batman and Robin. This has the potential to spin out of control. We need to put the brakes on this newfound partnership before they find out about our little agreement."

———

JANE GOLD WAS PACING IMPATIENTLY at the Bahnhof waiting for Drake to arrive. Looking at her watch, she wondered where the hell he was.

For the past twenty minutes, her phone had been pinging non-stop with the shocking news that the embassy was being closed and the staff deported. The last call had been from the ambassador himself and he pointedly asked Gold where Drake was. Gold claimed not to know anything, but Stokes was no fool. She knew he knew she was lying. Nobody was fooling anybody.

In the end, she switched her phone off hoping that

Drake wouldn't try to contact her. If the ambassador called again, she wasn't sure she could lie convincingly.

Damn you Charlie, she thought. You're going to sink my career. Where the hell are you?

———

THE NEWS that the entire US embassy staff in Berlin had been declared persona non grata sent shockwaves throughout the world, but mostly in Washington DC. President Galway never seriously thought that Meyer would go through with it and his threat to exhume Trent's body was merely a bluff. He knew it would be a waste of time. The toxin would be untraceable.

Now he had a dilemma. Should he retaliate by publicly accusing Germany of assassinating a sitting US president? The Secretary of State had warned Galway of the dangers of doing so without proper evidence to back up the allegations. Germany would almost certainly deny it and the EU would close ranks around one of their own. At a time when the new Galway administration needed their allies the most, alienating a large chunk of them would be an unmitigated disaster.

This was all on the mind of Galway as he walked from the private residence of the White House to the back door of the Oval Office. As he walked past the garden, he saw Director James Barton waiting for him, sitting pensively on a bench.

"Director Barton" said Galway, "come to take the weight of the world off my shoulders?"

Barton grimaced. "I try my best every day, but I'm afraid Lester has really landed us in it this time. Without publicly accusing the Germans of assassination, we are going to end up looking like the lawless bandits here, killing a senior German intelligence official."

"Secretary of State Braddock has already warned me not to accuse them" said Galway, "he says that without evidence, it will backfire in our faces."

"You're the President" said Barton, "it's up to you."

Galway paused. "Why do you support me when others don't? I've often wanted to ask."

Barton scratched his neck absently as he thought about it. "You were in an impossible situation when Trent died. As Vice-President, you were constitutionally obligated to take over as president. But you had very big shoes to fill. Trent was extremely popular with the military establishment and the intelligence community. Suddenly he's gone and now they have to deal with you. I sympathise."

"You're the director of national intelligence" pointed out Galway, "if the intelligence community dislikes me, you should be their cheerleader."

Barton grunted. "Will I tell you why I didn't like Trent? Because he was a racist son-of-a-bitch who only hired me when he was accused of only having old white men in his Cabinet. I was under no illusions. You're different. Besides, I respect the constitution. If it says you are the president, then you have my loyalty."

Galway suddenly felt absurdly grateful. "Thank you. Now the fact that you are sitting there tells me you have something to tell me."

"Sit down" said Barton quietly.

When Galway sat down on the bench beside him, Barton continued. "I think you will agree that this is spinning out of control. Murder, mayhem, and now a major US embassy closed. Our reputation is being damaged. Meyer has the upper hand."

"A very succinct assessment" nodded Galway, "and your suggestion for turning this around?"

"You've already given CIA station chief Charlie Drake permission to work with the German government to bring in Finn. I want your permission to kill Finn when we capture him."

"Kill him?"

Barton nodded. "Cut the head off the snake."

"We don't try to bring him in?"

"Do you really think that's wise Mr President? The Germans want to put him on trial. Under pressure, who knows what he will say? We can contain the Lester situation. If he wants a plea deal, he'll play along. But if Finn opens his mouth? Then it's game over. A CIA-sponsored assassination of a friendly nation intelligence official? People will never believe you didn't know about it and approve it."

"There's just one problem though" said Galway, "we have no idea where Finn is."

"Do you really think Lester is going to abandon his boy?" said Barton, "we've been monitoring his phones and he has been phoning an encrypted cell phone for days and getting no replies. But we cracked the encryption on that thing years ago and 'accidentally' forgot to tell the CIA. So we've been scooping up the voicemails he's been leaving, warning Finn that he was on borrowed time."

"Well then Finn will run" said Galway, suddenly dejected.

"He'll power up his phone eventually to get the messages" said Barton, "and when he does, we'll have his location. When we do, Drake puts a bullet in Finn and it's all over. His acolytes will either be killed, captured, or will scatter."

"You make it sound so easy" said Galway, a slight hint of sarcasm in his voice.

"Sometimes a person's downfall is that they overthink something which is actually very simple" said Barton calmly.

Galway stood up. "Then I spend the rest of my administration cleaning up the diplomatic side of things. Which won't be simple by any means. I will have to publicly prostrate myself in front of Meyer and suffer the consequences of Lester's decision forever."

"I can't help there unfortunately. I'm a spy, not a politician. So do I have your approval?"

Galway thought for a moment. "Yes, do it. Kill him. End this once and for all. Leave the diplomatic fallout to the Secretary of State and I."

Barton stood up and briskly shook Galway's hand. "Good decision sir. You can rely on me to get this done."

"Glad I can rely on someone around here" said Galway with a slight smile, who walked into the Oval Office where his next appointment was waiting.

Barton waited until Galway had closed the door to the Oval Office before taking out his phone and calling a German number.

"It's sanctioned" he said quietly, when it was picked up. "Put Finn in the ground. If anyone else gets in the way, put them down too."

CHAPTER FIFTEEN

Gold was about to lose her mind but her stress evaporated when Drake and Decker suddenly turned up at the Bahnhof as arranged.

"Where the hell have you been?" snapped Gold, "and why is *she* here?"

Decker smirked. "Glad to make your acquaintance Jane."

Drake held up a hand to stop a brewing war of the ladies. "The president has authorised us to work with Department 89 to put a stop to all of this. It was going to be the whole of Berlin CIA station, but with the closure of the embassy, this is going to be more like the A Team instead." He suddenly looked doubtful. "Or maybe the B Team."

"We have to work with Major Decker and her crew?" said Gold, "God give me strength."

Drake looked uncomfortable. "Actually that's acting BfV director Decker and her crew."

"What?" said Gold, looking shocked, "you've been given Wagner's job?"

"On a temporary basis" said Decker, "so let's cut the bullshit here, OK? You don't like me and I don't like you. Let's admit it and move on. Stop getting your panties in a twist. Temporarily our interests are aligned. You want Finn stopped and we want him for a trial. So let's work together on this."

"To put a fellow CIA agent on trial in a foreign country? No thanks. He's going back to the US for debriefing."

"Jane" said Drake quietly, "I think it's going to get to the stage where we will have to put Finn and his people down. They're out of control and refusing to back down."

"He was following the orders of Norman Lester" she protested, "he doesn't deserve to be executed."

"Look Jane, this is absurdly simple" said Drake patiently, "either you are on board and you help us, or you are on the next plane to Washington DC with the rest of the office. Your choice. Make it now."

Gold got her temper under control. "And what exactly are we supposed to do? We don't know where Finn and his merry band of renegades are. And with Berlin station shut down, we can forget about CIA resources."

"We have the President's authority" said Drake,

"which last I checked was good for something. We also have a name - Frank Dixon."

"And he is?"

"One of Finn's men who was shot dead killing Martin Lesch and who is currently lying in a morgue" said Decker, "Drake says you have a Langley contact who could look Dixon up?"

Gold glared. "Charlie talks too much."

"Can you make the call or not?" said Decker.

Gold got her phone out. "Give me a minute."

ON THE OTHER PLATFORM, Fawkes and Bailey were sitting on a bench watching Drake, Decker, and Gold. They had followed Drake and Decker from the Lesch assassination crime scene. Fawkes had a baseball cap on over his eyes and he chewed on gum, as he peered under the rim of the cap.

"They don't look too dangerous" he remarked to Bailey who was drinking coffee and fidgeting with a gun in his rain jacket pocket.

"Don't even think about it" said Bailey, "you heard Finn. Those three come last. We have plans for the other two first."

"Schmitz and Graf" said Fawkes, rolling the names over his tongue, "I hear Schmitz is a cripple. And the other's a blonde bimbo. Can't be too dangerous."

Bailey finished his coffee. "Well then we'll leave them to you then. Come on, they're leaving. We have to follow them."

DRAKE AND DECKER followed Gold out of the station but hung back while she made her call. When she was finished, she beckoned them over.

"Well, Finn certainly has friends in low places. This Frank Dixon has been connected to Finn for almost twelve years. An absolute scumbag. My contact says that the agency will be extremely pleased that Dixon is no longer breathing."

"Known associates?" said Drake.

"Just Finn. Other known associates are all confirmed dead."

"So how do you want to play this?" asked Drake to Decker.

Decker pulled out a phone from her pocket. "This is Dixon's. I took it from his pocket."

"You stole evidence" shot back Gold.

"So what?" replied Decker scornfully, "I am going to get my tech person to crack this open and see if we can trace any of the late Frank Dixon's scumbag friends."

PENELOPE BRINKMANN AWOKE from her drug-induced sleep and turned painfully in the bed. Her body was in pain but not as much as it would have been, if it wasn't for the morphine currently coursing its way through her body.

With shaking hands, she tried to grab the sides of the hospital bed and heave herself into a sitting position. Doing so caused her to gasp. Her heavily bandaged hip and leg started shaking and as she turned her head to the side, she saw Amsel lying in a hospital bed beside her. He was conscious, although it was obvious he had been badly wounded in the shoulder. The shoulder was encased in bandages and there was a sheen of sweat on his face.

"Amsel?" whispered Brinkmann, "what happened?"

Amsel grunted. "I was wondering when you would wake your lazy ass up. I got shot, just like you."

"Shot by who?"

"You've been asleep too long and therefore not up to date with the shit-show that has been going on" said Amsel, who proceeded to tell her everything that had happened.

When he was finished, he was startled to see Brinkmann struggling out of bed.

"Where the hell are you going in that condition?" he asked, astonished.

"Back to work" she said, gasping. Her legs felt like jelly and she felt lightheaded. "Assholes to kill."

"And what good do you think you'll be to anyone if you can hardly stand up?"

Brinkmann glared. "I was shot and my apartment ripped to shit. You think I am going to lie here, read trashy magazines and eat grapes while the people responsible are going round Berlin causing even more mayhem?"

Amsel sighed. "When you put it like that...."

He got out of bed himself, grimacing at the pain in his shoulder.

"What are *you* doing?" asked Brinkmann.

Amsel slowly reached for a shirt which was on the back of a chair. "Far be it from me to let a woman show me up."

Pulling on jeans, jackets, and shoes, they headed to the door only to be confronted by the doctor who looked at them enraged.

"And where the hell do you think you're going?" he said, pointing back to the beds.

"To kill assholes" they replied together, gently pushing past the doctor and limping out. Amsel and Brinkmann held onto one another as a wave of nausea and dizziness hit them both but they wisely kept that fact from the doctor, who was now phoning Schmitz in a pissed off rage.

WHEN BRINKMANN and Amsel staggered out of the elevator at Department 89 headquarters, they saw Graf standing there waiting, who was not happy.

"What the hell are you doing?" asked Graf coldly, "you two should be in a hospital."

"Funny, that" said Amsel, "the doctor asked us the same question and we said...."

"Yes, he told me what you said" interrupted Graf, "and somehow I think the assholes will be killing *you*. You can both barely stand up. Captain Schmitz is ordering you both to return to hospital."

"We respectfully decline" said Brinkmann, "we're not going to sit around in a bed while our friends are being attacked."

Graf sighed. "Yes, Schmitz and I knew that would be your answer. Sometimes you're both as bad as Decker."

"We'll take that as a compliment Sergeant" said Amsel, "now if you'll excuse me, I need to find a compliant and morally flexible department doctor to give Brinkmann and I very strong painkillers."

"Go to your offices" said Graf, "you'll find something to take the pain away sitting on your desks. Just don't overdo it."

A HOUR LATER, Schmitz and Graf saw Decker,

Drake, and Gold approaching from the other side of the Holocaust Memorial. Graf looked scornful.

"This is the sum total of our cooperation with the CIA? Two people?"

"You're forgetting Sergeant" said Schmitz, adjusting his cufflinks, "the US Embassy is closed. The CIA in Berlin has pretty much been decapitated for the time being. Those two are probably putting their careers on the line for us. Let's show them a little courtesy please."

Graf nodded without a word, as Decker raised a hand in greeting. Drake managed an uneasy smile. Graf scowled again and turned to scan the perimeter of the square.

"My dear leader" said Schmitz to Decker, "you're looking a little rough around the edges."

"Well we can't all be as dapper as you with your Walmart suit" said Drake.

"Hey, no Walmart here" protested Schmitz, "this is the real Italian deal I'm wearing."

Decker was not in the mood. "Boys, if you don't mind. We can discuss fashion later. Did you not bring Liebermann as I asked? I've got a phone here needing cracked."

"She's on her way" said Schmitz, "she's bringing the Batmobile with her."

The Batmobile was the fully-equipped tech van which enabled her to do her work while on the road.

"The Batmobile?" said Drake questioningly.

Decker shook her head. "You'll see."

———

ON THE OTHER side of the square, Fawkes and Bailey looked in disbelief at the sight of three senior Department 89 agents standing in the one place. It was almost as if Christmas had come early.

"Do we take them all now?" muttered Bailey.

Fawkes took out his phone. "Not without Finn's say-so which I'm going to get now."

Before he could dial, a dark van approached.

"Who the hell is this?" said Fawkes, unaware he was staring at the infamous Batmobile.

CHAPTER SIXTEEN

Sergeant Penelope Brinkmann carefully drove the van into the square and cut the engine. One of her techs, who was sitting in the back, could be heard slurping loudly from a plastic fast food cup of coke. Liebermann rolled her eyes. She really hated that guy. He was a slob.

She got out of the truck, making sure to put on her baseball cap and dark sunglasses first. Looking around, she saw Decker and the others waiting for her, and they walked up to her. She was not allowed to leave the van alone for a second. Too much valuable and sensitive equipment, and the guy in back would rather save his soda than the van.

"Major, Captain" nodded Liebermann, as they approached. Liebermann suddenly felt nervous, as she had heard from Schmitz that Decker was out for her blood. But Decker was for now acting normally, so Liebermann relaxed.

Decker handed her Dixon's phone. "I need you to crack this open and get the call history, contacts....you know the score. If there's any dirty pictures on there, I want to see them. Videos too."

She said the last two words with so much emphasis that Liebermann's blood pressure went up, and Schmitz discreetly cleared his throat. Graf, Drake, and Gold looked on wondering what the deal was.

"Yes Ma'am" stuttered Liebermann and she ducked inside the van. She had just built a new phone cracking tool and she was eager to try it out. She just had to get her slob of a tech guy moving on the job.

"Aseem!" she yelled, "put the soda down! Time to get to work!"

"THEY'RE WHAT?" said Finn in disbelief over the phone.

"They're all here in one place" said Fawkes, a manic grin on his face, "Decker the bitch, Schmitz the cripple, Graf the bimbo, two with CIA written all over them, and another blonde in a van."

"No nickname for the van blonde?" said Finn sarcastically.

"Give me time."

Finn thought furiously. "I'm only a half hour out. We can take them out in one shot, then be out of Germany tonight."

"They're not going to stick around forever" said Fawkes in a sing-song voice.

"I'm only a half hour away" repeated Finn, "I'll call Gardner and Cassidy and tell them to also make their way there. Until then, do not engage unless you see them leaving. Then do what you can to slow them down. Otherwise, wait for us. Decker is mine."

IN THE END, it took less than ten minutes for Liebermann to crack the phone's encryption and bypass the main PIN code.

"Major, Captain" she called, "I'm in."

The back door of the van opened and Decker and the others piled in. Aseem the tech looked uncomfortable at his personal space being invaded and he pushed himself into the corner, hugging his drink.

"There are various numbers in the call history" said Liebermann, "most likely burners. Wait...."

"What?" said Graf.

"According to the systems here, the phones are on. And.....the signal is coming from here."

"Here?" said Drake.

"They're outside" whispered Liebermann.

Decker and Schmitz edged to the back door, weapons in hand. But before they could open the door, there was a click and a pistol was pushed against Drake's head.

"Put the guns down, all of you" Gold said icily, "or what there is of Charlie Drake's brain will get sprayed over these fancy new computers."

"This is the second time today a woman has pushed a gun into my head" muttered Drake sullenly, "it's getting to be a bit of a bad habit."

"So much for trusting her" said Decker.

"Charlie was always gullible that way" laughed Gold, "weren't you dear? Always falling for the ones in short skirts and skimpy blouses?"

"You're working for Finn?" said Drake in a resigned tone of voice.

"Let's just say I have my loyalties in order" said Gold, "that's all you need to know. Unfortunately, my orders call for you to die. But take heart, you'll be dying for your country, and you'll get your star on the wall in the CIA lobby."

"Wonderful" said Drake, "just what I want after sixteen years of selfless service."

As Gold prepared to pull the trigger, Aseem the IT tech suddenly decided that his own self-preservation was at stake. So with a burst of bravado, he threw the cup of soda into Gold's face, while pushing the pistol away from Drake's head.

In the small compact space in the back of the van, it

was a miracle that nobody was shot. But there was a casualty. As Aseem and Gold struggled for control of the gun, the trigger was pulled and a bullet hit the phone cracking software sitting on the desk opposite.

Liebermann was furious.

"That was a one-off prototype!" she shrieked. With an eruption of fury, she grabbed the ruined device and swung it, intending to hit Gold across the jaw. But instead, she accidentally hit Drake in the face which made him slump to the ground in shock.

With her prisoner down, Gold was left exposed. This allowed Graf to get her arm around Gold's throat and snap her neck with a single movement. Gold's eyes rolled and she breathed a hissing sound as the breath left her lungs. Graf released her arm and Gold fell on top of an already stunned Drake.

"Call the number!" said Decker.

"What?" said Liebermann, confused.

"You said they're outside" said Decker, "so call the number. Let's see who picks up their phone."

With shaking hands, Liebermann dialled the number while Schmitz discreetly looked out of the van's driver-side window. He saw Fawkes and Bailey on the other side of the square as Fawkes took out his phone.

"Got you" said Schmitz, "let's go."

FAWKES HESITATED, which was his undoing.

He stared at the ringing phone, saw it was Dixon's number and momentarily couldn't comprehend how he was getting a call from a dead man.

But when the doors of the van opened and everyone came out with guns drawn, the penny finally dropped.

"Oh....shit" he said, mouth open. "Game on, I guess."

As he and Bailey pulled out their guns, the car containing Finn, Gardner, and Abney raced into the square. But it was too late for Bailey, as a sustained burst of machine gun fire from Drake lifted Bailey into the air and onto his back, a small sardonic grin on his face, as if he was telling a joke to the Devil.

"One down" said Drake with satisfaction.

Seeing Bailey down, Fawkes jumped behind one of the stone blocks of the Holocaust Memorial as bullets thudded into the stone. One bullet grazed his cheek which made him snarl in pain.

"Finn is not paying me enough for this shit!" he yelled, as screaming Berliners and tourists ran for cover.

———

AS THE CAR braked to a stop, Finn yanked open the passenger door and began firing in the direction of Decker and the others. He emptied the clip of his magazine, then rapidly reloaded as Schmitz and Graf opened fire back at the car.

This was bad for Abney who was in the driver's seat and hadn't managed to get out of the car yet. Struggling to get his seatbelt off, a well-aimed bullet from Graf's gun shattered the windshield and blew the top of Abney's head off. The blood hit Gardner who cursed as he struggled to get out of the back seat.

"We need to get out of here Finn" shouted Gardner as he uselessly wiped his face, "we're outgunned and the local cops will be here any minute."

"Not till they're dead" said Finn through gritted teeth, "stay on mission, or forget being paid."

"Damn" said Gardner, checking his weapon, "what's the point of money if you're not alive to enjoy it?"

Before Finn could reply, Gardner roared and started a volley of fire in the direction of the van which Decker and the others were hiding behind. Several of the bullets thudded harmlessly off the armour-plated surface but it made Decker and the others hide behind the vehicle for a moment.

"Now they'll think twice about sticking their heads out" said Gardner with satisfaction, "but they will still have called in reinforcements. We're on the clock now."

Finn opened up a satchel and produced several fragmentation grenades. "Then let's accelerate the timetable."

KATJA LIEBERMANN WAS TECHNICALLY NOT a soldier, having been drafted into Department 89 for her hacking skills. But she had had basic training, and once before, she had been forced to pick up a gun and fight. So as Gardner's bullets found their mark, disabling Liebermann's precious van, she got enraged.

Aseem, the IT tech, was in the corner, crouched beside the dead body of Gold. He was clutching his soda cup and looking terrified. Liebermann realised he was going to be no help and ran to the driver's seat.

"If you need a job done properly, you've got to do it yourself" she yelled.

Gunning the engine, she hit the accelerator and the van shot forward. This left the others behind the van completely exposed which made Schmitz curse out loud. But Decker smiled. She knew what Liebermann was about to do.

But Fawkes, who had been trying to sneak up on them, saw their sudden exposure out in the open, and laughed to himself, raising his gun.

"Christmas come early!" he said, "bye bye."

Two shots could be suddenly heard but not from Fawkes' gun. Instead blood blossomed on Fawkes's chest. He looked down uncomprehendingly at his wounds, then closed his eyes and slumped to the ground.

Behind him was Penelope Brinkmann, whose body was slumped to the side in pain. Next to her was Amsel.

"Got you, you son of a bitch" she gasped.

Before Decker and the others could say anything, a massive crash could be heard.

LIEBERMANN DIDN'T LIKE to reinvent the wheel. So when she saw a vehicle that needed taking out, and she was in a vehicle of her own...well the solution didn't need a fancy invention of its own.

Accelerating, she raced straight towards the car which Finn and Gardner were now behind. At that speed, she couldn't miss. A huge crunch of metal and Finn's small hire car was catapulted over several times like a crushed piece of cardboard.

Both Finn and Gardner, being at the back, were trapped. Behind them were the solid stones of the Holocaust Memorial, so they were trapped between the large stones and the car. As Liebermann's van smashed into the car, both Finn and Gardner were crushed in the middle like the meat in a sandwich.

Gardner was the most unfortunate one as the back of the car rolled over his body and over his head. He mercifully felt nothing as he died instantly. Finn on the other hand was pinned from the waist down, unable to move and in a tremendous amount of pain. He screamed as the back wheel and the wreckage of the back bumper rolled over his legs and pinned him down.

For a moment, the only sounds coming from the

square was screaming. Screaming from locals and tourists, and screaming from an extremely badly wounded Finn, uselessly flailing about under the wreckage of the car like a fish out of water. Brinkmann meanwhile staggered out of the driver's side of the van with a hysterical Aseem clutching his soda cup and laptop. Brinkmann was clutching a MP5 machine gun and was itching to use it.

Drake stood up along with the others in awe. "Well I'll be goddamned. I didn't see that coming."

"Never underestimate the quiet ones" said Decker, raising her weapon. She turned to Brinkmann and Amsel hobbling over. "So you got our SOS then?"

"Yes Major" said Amsel, "and Unterwald has stood down the police for the next fifteen minutes. So whatever has to be done, do it now."

Decker nodded. "Time to take out the trash."

CHAPTER SEVENTEEN

Finn had never known so much pain, and he was in no doubt that his back was broken. He could taste blood in his mouth and had trouble breathing.

But there was nothing wrong with his eyes, so when he saw Decker and the others approach, he knew he was in serious trouble. Looking around, he could see his gun but when he reached out for it, it was frustratingly out of reach. Just the act of reaching out his hand caused his body to rear up in agony. He placed his head back on the ground against fragments of glass from the car.

Decker approached the overturned vehicle. In her hand was two of the fragmentation grenades which Finn was about to throw at them and never had the chance.

"I think you dropped something" she said.

Finn looked anxiously at Decker then suddenly started laughing uncontrollably.

"Did I tell a joke?" said Decker, coldly.

"You're the joke" wheezed Finn, "a woman in a man's job with all your compliant slaves following your every whim."

"I'm the joke? I'm not the one under an overturned vehicle, his body crushed, about to die."

Finn grunted. "I'm not afraid of dying. I was merely following orders. As a German, you should be familiar with that concept."

"Ten minutes" murmured Amsel.

Decker leaned down and pulled the pins on both grenades. She then stuffed them inside Finn's trousers next to his groin.

"This is for Klaus Wagner" she said, who then turned and walked away slowly. The others meanwhile were running fast, yelling at Decker to move faster.

Finn looked with horror at his groin as he realised what was going to happen. He then suddenly stopped and closed his eyes, resigning himself to his fate.

The explosion when it came was tremendous. The remaining petrol in the car tank ignited, sparking a fireball. The smouldering metal of the car was lifted into the air by the force of the blast, and Finn was incinerated.

As for the Holocaust Memorial, it was virtually destroyed as chunks of stone rained down on everyone in the square.

As the explosion went down, Schmitz staggered to his

feet, his ears ringing. He looked down to see a huge hole in the new trousers of his suit.

"I've had this suit for two days!" he shouted, "this is going on expenses!"

TEN MINUTES LATER, the police arrived headed by Chief Inspector Otto Busch. When Busch saw the devastation, he seriously started thinking about early retirement.

"What is it about you and chaos?" he asked Decker, "everywhere you go, disaster follows."

"Story of my life" said Decker, who wearily got into a government car and was driven away at high speed.

"Left to clean up the mess again" sighed Busch. "What a life."

IT DIDN'T TAKE LONG for the incident to make its way onto the evening news and Peter Humphries sat in his office in the British Embassy looking forlorn. He knew it was only a matter of time before Decker put two and two together.

As if on cue, his phone rang.

"Mr Humphries" said Decker, "I believe I told you to stay in touch."

"I've nothing to share Major."

"Well I do. Chief of Staff Unterwald's office in thirty minutes. Don't make me come and get you."

FIFTEEN MINUTES LATER, Humphries was admitted to Unterwald's office. He saw a very chilly looking Unterwald sitting behind his desk, with Decker standing impassively in the corner of the room.

"Well, I'm here" said Humphries, "what is it?"

Unterwald stood up and buttoned his jacket.

"Peter Humphries, due to a serious violation of diplomatic protocol, as of now, you have been declared 'persona non grata' in the Federal Republic of Germany. You have forty-eight hours to get out."

Humphries stood for a moment, unable to comprehend.

"Why?" he said eventually, "I deserve a real reason."

Unterwald looked at Decker, who was taking a phone out of her pocket.

"Guess whose phone this is" said Decker.

"I can't begin to guess."

"Jane Gold, now-deceased deputy CIA chief of station."

Humphries struggled to keep a straight look on his face. "OK. So what?"

"Take a wild guess whose number she has on speed dial. The same number she was also taking calls from immediately after Martin Lesch's assassination?"

No answer.

"Nothing to say Mr Humphries? Why don't we dial the number and see if we can hear the other phone ringing?"

"Fine" he snapped, "let's cut the bullshit. It's mine. So what? We were both spooks. Colleagues. There's nothing out of the ordinary about that."

"No" conceded Decker, "but I'm sure you'll agree this is out of the ordinary."

Decker pulled up a leather bag from the side of a chair, and spilled out the contents to reveal huge bundles of used banknotes. They covered all of Unterwald's desk.

"We pulled Lesch's bank statements. He was up to his neck in debt. Literally drowning due to bad investments. Then suddenly he gets a large payment from a shell company in the Bahamas which pays back half of what he owed. We were at his house today and we ripped it apart, and we found all this money behind the wall. A hundred thousand Euros. Fancy that."

"I'm still waiting for the part where you connect me to all of this" said Humphries menacingly.

"I think you and Gold found out that Lesch was drowning in debt and decided to carry out a joint UK-US operation to recruit him. Secrets in exchange for cash.

But Lesch eventually wanted out and you went to meet him at his speech to try and talk him out of it. But he was assassinated before you could talk to him."

"Like I said" said Humphries, "prove it."

Unterwald took a small tape recorder out of his desk.

"We will" he said, "when Lesch decided he wanted out, he decided to start tape recording his conversations with you. Care to hear some?"

Without waiting for a reply, Unterwald pressed the play button and Humphries' voice could be heard.

"You simply can't just leave Mr Lesch. You took our money."
"Which was earned. I gave you intelligence material. We're even."
"I'll tell you when we're even. Or would you like Chancellor Meyer to know you're a traitor?"

Unterwald switched off the recorder to see that the fight had left Humphries. He looked defeated.

"The bastard taped me" he muttered.

"Pack your things and get out of the country Mr Humphries. Nobody recruits our ministers as spies and expects to be forgiven. Especially nations we assume are our friends."

WHEN HUMPHRIES HAD BEEN ESCORTED out, Decker looked at Unterwald.

"I'd like a word with the Chancellor please."

Unterwald nodded and took her down the hallway to her office suite. Breezing past the secretary, he knocked on Meyer's door and went in without waiting for a reply.

Meyer was on the phone, her stocking feet up on her desk. When she saw Unterwald and Decker, she nodded and held up a finger to indicate she would be just another minute.

When she eventually got off the phone, she got up and poured generous drinks for the three of them.

"Here's to the successful conclusion of another operation" she said.

"You've heard about Martin Lesch?" said Decker.

"That he was a British and American agent?" said Meyer, "yes I'm afraid to say that piece of bad news reached my ears. Of course the public will never hear of it."

"I've come to request that I be relieved of my duties as acting BfV director" said Decker, "I want to return to Department 89. The BfV is too big and bureaucratic for me. You know I wouldn't last."

Meyer looked at her for a long moment. "I suppose you're right. You're better at dealing with the unmentionables and staying in the shadows. Fine, I'll ask Unterwald to come up with candidates for Wagner's replacement. Don't worry, it'll be somebody well deserving of the job."

"I ask for nothing more Madam Chancellor" said Decker, saluting.

CHAPTER EIGHTEEN

In Washington DC, the 'Berlin Affair' as it was being called by a very unimaginative cable news media, was exploding even further. The news of the ferocious gun battle and explosion ending in the deaths of Finn and his rogue agents sullied Langley's reputation. Congress was demanding hearings and heads to roll.

Galway was only too happy to serve up Norman Lester and deny responsibility. On the advice of his Secretary of State, he had decided not to publicly accuse Germany of assassinating Trent. They would never be able to prove it and it would just make an already bad situation even worse.

Galway was sitting in the Oval Office late at night when there was a knock on the door and Barton looked in.

"Mr President? You have a moment for me?"

Galway looked exhausted. He loosened off his tie and waved Barton in.

"Everyone else wants a piece of me, so you may as well have your turn."

Barton nodded grimly and sat down on the couch.

"I think we can safely say we have the situation contained" he said.

Galway barked a short laugh. "Contained? That's what you call it? I have the Speaker calling for me to resign. That's when he's not frantically looking for microphones to demand hearings. Lester's attorneys are going on TV loudly exclaiming that I promised a sweetheart deal in exchange for his cooperation. And our relations with Germany and the rest of the EU will take years to repair. So please Director Barton, tell me what part is contained?"

"Finn and the others are dead. You can now focus on clean-up and damage control."

"Or my successor can focus on it. I'm not sure if I can survive this. If I knew about this in advance, I am a raging psychopath. If I didn't know about it, I am embarrassingly incompetent. I can't win."

"It's all a matter of what people can prove" said Barton calmly, "and they can't prove shit. You just say Lester did this on his own, deny the sweetheart deal, and order the Attorney-General to nail Lester to the wall."

"Make him the sacrificial lamb."

"Better you than him" shrugged Barton, "unless you really want to quit?"

"No, I don't" said Galway, his shoulders sagging, "Until all of this, I was starting to get used to the job."

"Then tell the Speaker where he can stick his resignation demands. And his hearings."

Galway made a decision. "I want you to become the next director of the CIA. I need someone I can trust over there, someone who doesn't get fazed easily. There's a lot of rebuilding to be done. I can't think of anyone better to do it."

Barton contemplated the idea. "OK" he said, finally "but only if you don't quit. If you go, I go too."

Galway wearily held out a hand. "Deal."

As Barton prepared to go, his mobile phone rang.

"Barton.....when? Oh dear God, I thought he was being watched? Fine, but this isn't over. I'll call you back."

Hanging up, he looked at Galway. "Lester is dead. He committed suicide by hanging himself in his bathroom. Suicide letter, the lot."

"Tell me we didn't do this to him."

"No we didn't" said Barton, "he did this to himself. See? Things are getting better with every passing minute."

BRINKMANN AND AMSEL were told they were in for an extended period of physiotherapy, and in Brinkmann's case, also psychotherapy. This prompted her to swear loudly that she didn't want to see "any goddamn shrink" but Decker put her foot down and that was that.

One day, when both Brinkmann and Amsel were in the gym trying desperately to get themselves back to operational fitness, Schmitz walked in.

"Lieutenant Amsel, you're finished for the day. I need to speak to Sergeant Brinkmann."

Amsel looked at them both. "OK. I'm obviously being cut of a loop here but that's fine." He picked up his towel and painfully limped out of the gym.

"Look, if this is about the shrink...." began Brinkmann.

"No" interrupted Schmitz, "it's about you and Decker."

"I'm not sure I know what you mean."

"Sergeant, your loyalty is admirable, but please do not insult my intelligence again" snapped Schmitz, "I've seen the video footage from outside your apartment at 2.30am the night before your attack. You and the Major necking against the wall. I've spoken to the Major and she knows that she has made a very serious mistake."

Brinkmann smarted. "So.....what? You're the messenger telling me to back off and leave things alone?"

Schmitz looked livid. "Watch your tongue Sergeant. I am trying to save both your careers. If the Chancellor heard about this, you'd both be done. You'd be reduced to flipping burgers in a fast food joint."

"What do you need me to say?" said Brinkmann eventually.

"That you understand this goes no further and you develop permanent amnesia about that night."

Brinkmann swallowed several times. "You've got it."

"Good" said Schmitz, "take the rest of the day off."

DECKER WAS in her office when a confidential "eyes only" message came in for her. When she ripped the envelope open, she realised the message was from an unexpected source, sent through back channels.

"I hear our American friends have discovered what happened to President Trent in Malaysia. That is unfortunate. I hope our secret about me is safe. I am quite enjoying being leader of North Korea."

"Don't worry Myong" murmured Decker, "you're safe. I'll make sure of it."

DID YOU ENJOY THIS BOOK?

I would greatly appreciate it if you would leave a

honest review of this book online. Reviews are what drives sales, so they are very important for me. But getting those reviews are extremely hard. Many people don't bother, but without them, my work will sink without trace!

Remember, you have the power to make or break this book by saying what you think. Whether the review is positive or negative, it doesn't matter. I love hearing what my readers thought of my work and I will try to read every review.

Simply go here - https://books2read.com/opthunderbolt and click on the button to the store where you bought this book from. Then leave your review.

If you want to, you can also send me an email at publishing@markoneill.org, and tell me your thoughts and feedback. I can't guarantee a reply, but I will certainly try my best, time permitting.

I OCCASIONALLY SEND out an email newsletter with information on upcoming new releases, as well as special offers.

If you sign up to the mailing list, you will receive advance notice of new books coming out, so you can grab them at the cheaper introductory price. You will also get subscriber-only special deals, such as exclusive free sample chapters, offers of free books from other recommended independent authors, and other goodies as I think of them.

If you are interested, you can sign up at https://signup.markoneill.org. You can easily unsubscribe at any time, and you have my personal guarantee that at no time will your personal details be sold to a third-party.

ABOUT THE AUTHOR

Mark O'Neill is a 40-something Scotsman, now living in Würzburg, Germany. Since 2004, he has been a technology journalist, editor, ghostwriter and copywriter.

He has also advised companies on implementing social media strategies and how to improve workplace productivity using technology.

When he is not writing, Mark likes to read, collect books, scour the Internet for story ideas, and discuss politics. But all of that is secondary to spending time with his wife and dog whom he adores.

You can visit Mark on the web at https://www.markoneill.org and https://www.department89.com

facebook.com/markoneillonline

twitter.com/markoneill

instagram.com/markoneill_author

amazon.com/author/markoneill

goodreads.com/markoneill

bookbub.com/profile/mark-o-neill

Printed in Great Britain
by Amazon